Everything I Learned by Age 40

G.W. Clift

Woodley Memorial Press

Mr. Clift wishes to thank Mr. Gary Lechliter for guiding this collection through publication and Mr. David Mayes for the cover photographs.

ISBN: 978-0-9828752-6-1

"Great Plain" previously appeared in *North American Review*, "Pharmacology" in *Uncle*, "Ode" in *The Pittsburgh Quarterly Review*, "Center for Advanced Thought" in *Amarillo Bay*, "The Spirit Photograph" in *South Dakota Review*, "Additional Material for Dick Francis's Dead Cert" in *Project for a New Mythology*,, "To Claim Your Prize" in *The Same*, and "Notes for Jim's Eulogy" in *A Summer's Reading*.

Everything I Learned by Age Forty

—for Johnny

The Spirit Photograph

After the now utterly gray-haired Everett recovered from the operation on his leg and returned to his shop, the regulars talked him into calling his alma mater and ordering in a second barber.

They had all gotten shaggy during his recuperation and they assured Everett that there was enough business in Forsythe and Morrill County to warrant someone tending to customers in the second chair that had been unmanned since old Paul McGillivray's death two years earlier.

Without any prefatory remarks, the young woman first took her place behind that chair on the Tuesday after she received her diploma at Topeka Barber College. Totally professional she looked in the relative brightness of the shop light—no jewelry, straight black hair, shining clean and cut at shoulder length (neatly done, but without any pretense to art), a clean white smock worn over a very simple skirt and plain, flat-heeled shoes, and with the tools of her adopted trade clean and arrayed on the shelf along beside her sink—not too many of them but not too few, either. It was a dark and rainy morning, the gray storm clouds skulking close to the horizon in every direction from the little prairie town. Three substantial pickup trucks sat parked diagonally in front of the Acropolis Coffee Shop across the way from the barber's, but the streets themselves were quiet. Everett, uncomfortable, flicked on the high mounted television (so that the Weather Channel played there silently) and began re-stocking paper collar shields and clean towels, tootsie pops and the new magazines (though putting out the Playboy made him extremely uneasy) and so on, all the while hoping he was suggesting the right and friendly things about himself to the small person he hoped was to share his business.

"Morning, Dukey," Everett said. "The new barber's here." He indicated the oriental woman. "Miss Mai Kato—have I got that right?"

"Pleased to meet you," Dukey said. He caught himself about to offer her a hand to shake, stole a glance at her, and instead nodded his head slowly a couple of times and smiled. "Welcome to Forsythe. Are you from Asia someplace?"

"I graduated from Wichita West High School," she said in a soft voice, her pronunciation betraying the implications of her statement and her tone giving nothing else away. She just very faintly returned his smile.

Dukey nodded, embarrassed.

"Well, why don't you give yourself the honor of being her first customer?" Everett said, gesturing Dukey into the number two chair.

The hulking old cowboy bent at the knees, lowering his seat farther and farther until eventually he found the chair bottom. "I'd like a trim, please," he told Mai Kato, almost confidentially.

She began washing her hands, and Dukey looked quizzically to Everett, who raised his shoulders in a shrug, having not been able to get four complete sentences out of Mai Kato during their two brief conversations. If the old timers could get her to speak, her talk might reveal a little more about her. They wanted to be friendly.

As the hair cutting began, Everett propped himself up in one of the green waiting chairs and, over and around an open newspaper, watched the mirrored reflection of Mai Kato's progress. To keep the possibility of talk current, he said, "Here's a story about Pizza Hut International in the paper. They've had some trouble in some of the old eastern block countries and in Africa. Says the chain only succeeds in Western Europe, where there is a middle class prepared for it, and where they have all sorts of ways of advertising. Same sort of ads as here." He looked over the paper at Dukey, who sat popeyed, and Mai Kato, who was working very intently on a patch of grizzled hair over the customer's left ear.

"I can't help but think all the big American corporations are going to have to make everybody in the world just like us if they're going to sell to 'em."

Then in came another of the shop's familiars, a man almost as door-filling as Dukey, but much less laconic than the rancher. "Ah, the new barber," he said, smiling broadly. "Welcome. Welcome. I'm Hood Robinson."

"Bank president," Dukey explained, unasked, to the woman cutting his hair.

Mai Kato nodded to Mr. Robinson.

"I heard you were moving in to the Thirkell's apartment. That ought to be a nice place. Just come to town yesterday?"

She nodded again, her attention still apparently fixed on the hair over Dukey's ear.

"Moved in yesterday afternoon," Everett explained.

"Has somebody shown you the town?" Hood asked, settling into Everett's barber chair.

"Miriam Vanbenscoten," Mai Kato said in the soft little voice. She adjusted the position of Dukey's head. He blushed.

"Oh, you know Miriam?" Hood asked, hanging up his hat and coat. "Of course, she lives next door, and was probably very happy to see another young woman moving to town."

Little Forsythe and the county had long suffered from rural decline caused primarily by the automation of farming and even ranching and by the depression in domestic oil production. Ordinarily only about six of its high school's annual graduating class of thirty could find employment close enough to stay in the area. And so there weren't very many young single women living in town. Miriam had bought the abstracting and insurance office two years before, on the completion of her Sociology B.S. at K-State.

"Miriam took her out to eat at Lucinda's," Everett told the balding Hood. "And I took her over to the Acrop for breakfast. So she knows she'll have to do her own cooking."

Robinson and the older barber immediately turned their heads to see Mai's reaction to this, a version of the standing local joke about the quality of the town's eateries. Dukey threw his eyes to the right, trying to see her face without moving his head.

She simply went on carefully snipping away.

"Hope your dinner didn't give you heartburn," Hood said.

3

She smiled and shook her head without taking her eyes off Dukey's right sideburn. "Relax, please," she said to her customer, whose shoulders had risen to tense near his ear lobes. She stroked the base of his neck once, twice, and Dukey felt his stomach and back loosen to comfort.

Then in from the rain came hairless Coach Proctor, a retired man who liked to loaf in the shop. He was wearing black "referee" shoes and a sweatshirt in the front pouch of which he kept his hands, even when he sprawled in one of the waiting chairs. "Ev. Hood. Dukey. New barber?"

"Miss Mai Kato," Everett said. "This is Douglas Proctor who used to be the basketball coach at the high school."

"We usually have pretty good teams. Do you like basketball?" Hood asked the young barber.

"I was the boys' coach, a course," Mr. Proctor told her. "The thing of it is, we didn't even have girls teams again, or at least not traveling teams until the 1970s." He paused, waiting for her to comment. She said nothing. "Not that I have anything against girls' basketball, a course. But it is different. I think the girls are rougher—I think the refs let 'em play rougher, don't you know?"

Everett looked up from buzzing the bottom line on the back of Hood's neck to see what Mai would say. She didn't speak, but Ev's attention soon drifted to Dukey's appearance. Though his haircut wasn't yet finished, the cattleman looked fifteen years younger and ten pounds lighter. She's a terrific haircutter, Everett thought to himself. This is wonderful.

Still, within two minutes the conversation was about the weather. They hadn't been able to find anything less than a direct personal question that would make Mai Kato say a complete sentence. And when each man had commented, with undisguised surprise, on how good Dukey looked after the trim, she had turned away and begun washing her hands again.

Lanky E.Q. Dalquist, Miriam Vanbenscoten's fiance, came in about midmorning wearing a new pair of Wrangler jeans and asked Ev to use his sharpest scissors to cut the leather, brand-bearing belt loop off them for him. E.Q. owned a vast wheat farm in the west of the county on which he worked extremely hard about three weeks of every year. The rest of the time he wandered from his usual place at the counter of the Acropolis to his sweetheart's place of business to one of the two local bars (where he liked to play pool nearly every afternoon) to the barbershop. And he had a wheat farmer's way with a story. But Mai Kato seemed as oblivious to his conversation as politeness would allow while she worked over his wavy hair. The result of her professional attentions was so pronounced, made such an improvement in E.Q.'s appearance, that it prompted adulatory comments from Ev and Frank and Mrs. Shippen, who came in to post a xeroxed advertisement for an upcoming community theater performance of The Foreigner. Mrs. Shippen promised to send her husband in for a session with the new barber and went away down the street muttering to herself about how young and well-groomed E.Q. looked after Mai did his hair.

The new barber's reputation as an improver of masculine appearances spread around the town, and Everett, far from feeling jealous, enjoyed his business's renewed reputation and growing clientele. While men whose hair he had cut from their infancy to deepest middle age sat in the shop, waiting to have their looks rejuvenated and refined by the new barber, the proprietor took extra care to sweep and mop and dust, to sort and stock and wash everything in the shop, so that it soon looked its best, too. He bought new, "contemporary: design" client sheets and had the sign on the shop window repainted (professionally) for the first time in thirty years.

"How's that?" he asked Mai as she washed her hands between customers.

She looked at the new sign—The City Park Barbershop—and said, "Very nice." Her tone was kind, but she didn't smile. Ev wondered what she really thought.

After two weeks of nothing beyond the minimum of polite conversation with his new daily companion, the older barber still knew nothing about her or how she was enjoying her new life, and he had been unable to find the way to get her talking. Ev asked his next door neighbor of fifty-some years, Frank Pearl, to stop by for a Mai Kato haircut. The idea was for Frank to ask her to tell him a little about herself, about her tastes and opinions if not about her past. Hopefully Frank, a retired dentist, could draw her out.

"So," Frank said, relaxing into Mai's chair, the leather upholstery of its pads supple and shiny from the recent near constant use. "I live over by Everett. That's Gardener Street, over by the Maestro and all. Have Ev and Lottie had you over?"

"Please," she said, turning his head a little to one side.

"It's a nice old house. Well, how do you like your apartment?" Frank continued.

"It is very comfortable," she told him.

"Like your place in Topeka? he "asked.

"Yes," she said, buzzing off a neat line along the bottom of one sideburn.

Frank didn't want to be asking her a battery of direct questions but didn't know how else to proceed. "Whereabouts in Topeka did you live? I've got a niece lives there."

"Near the school." She set down the clippers and picked up her scissors. She tilted Frank's head upright. Then she began combing and snipping the hair around his crown.

"I've always got a little cowlick back there, even with the hair as thin as it's gotten..." Frank admitted before Ev caught his eye, and he remembered his object. "So you lived downtown in Topeka? Did you find that a little hairy? Sorry. I mean, given all the crime and the traffic and everything, weren't you nervous living down there?"

There was a brief pause before she answered. "No," she said.

Frank looked up for a cue from Everett but in the process glanced into the mirror. "My cowlick," he said, surprised. "Did you wet it down?"

"She didn't use any water," said Coach Proctor, who had been watching the haircut over an opened copy of the *Sports*

Illustrated swimming suit issue. "I was looking. She cut just a little and brushed with her hand and the thing disappeared."

Frank was surprised and elated. "It's gone. Ev, it's gone. I've hated that thing forever. Couldn't hold it down even with butch wax. And now all of a sudden it's gone."

Then Everett knew Frank wasn't going to come any closer to learning about Mai Kato's personal history than he already had. Oh, before Doc Pearl took his place in the chair Frank would remember himself and make another try at reestablishing his inquiry, but her monosyllabic replies had him back to praising her skills and referring to the weather within minutes.

Nobody had any luck getting Mai Kato to talk about herself, though every man in the county who had any hair left at all tried to draw her out during the first couple of months she was working in the shop. When he saw the slightly dingy Miriam Vanbenscoten in the canned vegetables aisle of the IGA one evening, Ev even asked her what she knew about the young barber. Miriam had been spending with the newcomer whatever time she didn't reluctantly devote to her abstracting and insurance businesses or, with rather more enthusiasm, to her romance with E.Q.

"I don't know anything about her, really," Miriam told Ev as she rubbed the temporary tattoo of a unicorn that graced her left biceps. "I like her. She's a good listener. But she doesn't say much."

"Well, where does she like to go? What does she like to do?"

Miriam leaned over her cart's handle. "Whenever we're together she sort of goes along with whatever I've thought up. We fiddled around with crystals one night. We rent movies sometimes. I've taken her bowling. But she never seems to have strong opinions about what we do."

"Is she reading anything? You've been over to her apartment. What's she got going on over there?"

Miriam thought. "She has a camera. And she likes to check books about photography out from the library, one at a time.

I'd read a magazine article about spirit photographs, about how you can get a photo of the aura of somebody, rather than of their physical appearances, and I was trying to explain that to her the other night, but she didn't seem interested." Miriam shook her head. "But she's pretty sweet. Or at least she doesn't actively avoid stuff I'd think would bore her. You know what I mean? I took her to a pancake feed at the church, and she got introduced to about twenty older ladies, and she just smiled and nodded all the way through. She didn't seem to be in any hurry to get out."

The next day Miriam watched Mai for signs of secretiveness. At lunch in the Acropolis on Thursday she noticed that though the newcomer rarely initiated any conversation, she spoke (albeit very, very quietly) to everyone in the coffee shop who spoke to her. When the two young women went for an evening walk once around the old International Harvester dealership, Miriam noticed that her friend didn't answer any question with more than the simplest possible answer that ordinary graciousness would require. But Mai did smile and nod along and even occasionally fill pauses in Miriam's musings with questions which prompted further telling. And later, back at Miriam's partially converted barn apartment, the new barber was nice to E.Q. when he arrived. But not too nice. And she left for her own place just after ten, at just about the right time.

Miriam took Mai to see the Friday night performance of the play (E.Q. not being much of a one for the theater). During the intermission, half the audience stepped out to enjoy the breeze from the sidewalk in front of the red brick high school auditorium which the community theater used. Once Mai Kato had disappeared into the Ladies Room ("to wash her hands," the abstracter would explain), Miriam conferred with Hood Robinson and Ev.

Hood asked. "How's our new resident doing? Does she seem to be happy?"

Everett and Miriam could only reply with shrugs.

"She hasn't been complaining, has she?"

"No," Evett admitted. "She never says anything to suggest she's unhappy or discouraged."

"I wonder if she feels properly welcomed," Hood mused aloud, stroking his chin.

"She actually seems a little embarrassed when people praise her haircuts," Ev said, "as they often do. I've been thinking about offering her a little raise just to make my appreciation of her work more obvious."

"Good," Hood said. Then he turned to Miriam. "Now, does she seem lonely? Have you been finding dates for her?"

"I wouldn't have any notion who she'd be compatible with," Miriam explained.

"Aren't you two spending a lot of time together?" Hood asked. "Somebody talky? Somebody who takes the initiative?"

"Who do you know who takes the initiative and yet needs me to fix him up with a date?" Miriam asked.

It was another week before they got a tip about their new friend from the newspaper. The usual column by Angelica Rentz, the county extension agent, included a paragraph congratulating Mai for winning second prize in a statewide photography contest she had entered soon after her arrival in Forsythe.

"Hey," Ev said when he read the column. He was sitting in his chair, whiling away a late afternoon as Mai tried to do something with the appearance of the high school basketball team's squirrelly off guard, a square-headed farm boy named Matthew Link. "Congratulations, Mai," the older barber said, and he read the news to her and noticed she was a little embarrassed. She may have even blushed.

"When do we get to see the prize winning picture?" he asked her.

But before she could answer, in came Hood Robinson, carrying the newspaper in his hand. "Congratulations," he said. And then here came the Mannerly Brothers, Toffee and Evan, leaving their haberdashery untended to pop in with the paragraph about the contest. And then Clement Muir and Mrs. Shippen.

When Mai arrived home after the impromptu party at the shop, she found Mrs. Thirkell had clipped the column and stuck it in her apartment's screen door.

"Hello, fellow shutterbug," E.Q. said, swinging into the barbershop half an hour after its opening the next morning. He had a family heirloom 35 millimeter camera in its hard leather case slung around his neck.

Mai nodded to him with what might have been a faint smile and then returned to work on what was left of Rev. Canty's hair.

Seated in the waiting chairs under the long mirror were Hood Robinson, Frank Pearl, Mr. and Mrs. Shippen, Everett, and Miriam, each one holding a camera of some sort. E.Q. saw them and was momentarily taken aback.

"What kept you?" Miriam asked him sarcastically. She had a vintage, pink plastic Kodak.

Before he could answer, big Dukey Gorman walked by, looked in and said, "Cheese."

"It was funnier the first two times," hollered Hood, getting up furious as Dukey disappeared from view.

E.Q. remembered the packet in his coat pocket. "I've got the prints," he announced.

Everyone crowded around (except Mai and the Reverend, though the latter craned his neck in an attempt to see the pictures through a gap in the huddle under Frank's right elbow). E.Q. had just picked the photos up at the extension office.

"Landscapes," said Hood, modestly surprised. There were no recognizable humans in any of the half dozen shots. The only individuals appeared in dark silhouette. Instead of concentrating on humans or their products, the black and white pictures were of the relatively flat high plains, the topography of the barbershop crowd's native area, and of the huge sky above.

Everett looked at one after another of the prints and saw nothing remarkable in the subjects. Nothing. "But look at how they catch the light," he said, almost hopefully.

"Yes," agreed Hood, who was also looking for something to praise, something to like, something that indicated the young barber's interests and tastes. "Gives the bluestem a heft."

Miriam agreed. "It sort of merges the vegetation and shadow to make the range look different." She shifted through a couple of the photos. "Yes. Yes."

"I like them," Toffee Mannerly said. "The shape of the land—it's beautiful."

By now they were all looking at the pictures and then turning to smile at Mai and nod. Very nice indeed.

"Did you develop these yourself?" Everett asked. "Do you have a dark room in your apartment?"

Mai looked up through her bangs.

"No," she explained. "The druggist had the prints made for me."

"Too bad," continued Ev, holding up a couple of the pictures. "If you're really interested in photography, you ought to have your own dark room. Do you know how to develop them?"

"Yes," she admitted. "But I do not have an enlarger."

Ev's and Hood's eyes met.

"You know, we ought to have a dark room we can all use," the banker said.

"Especially as we're all so into photography," Miriam said. Then she asked Everett, "Do you guys have a copy of the new *Photoplay* around here anywhere?" and began sorting through the contents of the magazine rack.

Over the next couple of days, photography was the subject around the shop. Frank brought in some old snapshots, made with one of those cameras into which one loads treated plastic daisy wheels instead of film, and asked Mai for advice about improving his "pix."

Maintaining her sobriety and speaking just a few words, she suggested that he concentrate on framing his shots, and in fact the top of his wife's head did not appear in any of the twenty -four prints. E.Q. and Miriam invited Mai over to the latter's apartment one evening to supervise a shoot of Miriam in a series of brightly colored bikinis, always lit by every lamp in the place, all arranged to broadcast on a pile of sand E.Q. had shoveled in that afternoon up against a sky blue cinder block wall. At the shop Ev took his Polaroid out after every haircut and captured every one of Mai's customers as they got up from the low-set barber chair. Dukey correctly identified his own pasture in the prize-winning pictures when they were printed in the twice-weekly official county newspaper. Then he stepped into the shop and told Mai to feel free to go out picture taking on his lease land any time she wanted. She helped Evan Mannerly load the film in his new all-automatic camera. Two times.

And then Ev put forward the idea of a "City Park Barbershop Photographers" club. Members could display their best pictures in the shop and would be welcome to use the darkroom that was to be retrofitted into the old bathroom back behind the partition. The developing supplies would be paid for by an annual subscription, though Ev himself and the bank would put up the money to buy the darkroom equipment.

"Would you mind going to the photography store in Topeka some Monday?" Ev asked Mai during a Thursday afternoon lull in business, "and picking up what all we'll need for the darkroom? You know, all the equipment and the pans and chemicals and papers and so on? We can have a cashier's check ready for you to take along to pay."

She quietly agreed, and the next day E.Q. and Miriam signed on to assist her. They would travel in the Dalquist truck. "Bring your camera," Miriam suggested. "We might see something to take a picture of."

The Monday of the trip was gray. Miriam, sitting in the middle of the pickup's cab, sensed E.Q.'s excitement as the miles of prairie rolled by to the tune of country stations represented by push buttons on the truck's radio so that the morning began with the button closest to the driver and progressed with eastward travel to the next to closest button and so on. Perusing a sale insert from the Topeka paper, Miriam checked off items they would be purchasing, reading the features and prices aloud and encouraging Mai to explain how each item figured in the development process. And they watched the Coca Cola signs pass, first just one here and there on an old laundromat or a pop machine, but then more and more

12

coming with ever increasing frequency as they approached population centers, on billboards and trucks and window banners and clocks and once on a giant tethered balloon of a Coke bottle, feminine curves and masculine erectness, until all the occurrences became repetitions of a white script highway mantra, repeated faster and faster and faster.

As they approached the capital, Miriam sensed that E.Q. was tensing. The songs on the radio became weepier and the conventional distances between cars shorter. Great lines of vehicles would be turning off for this shopping destination or that one, or for this huge office complex or that one. McDonald's billboards regularly insisted on certain routes. Along the way were strip shopping centers with stores devoted exclusively to the sale of greeting cards and with chain delicatessens and chain banks. And then downtown Topeka, its insufficiently redeveloped commercial district of five and six story buildings. And under the great black and white and red Microsoft sale sign, the photography store.

Getting out of the truck, E.Q. walked with a stiff bowleggedness that Miriam had not seen before. She followed him quickly, unused to unaccompanied exposure on the city streets.

Inside the large store, its headroom lifted visually by a disorganized collection of high hung ad banners, Mai took charge. She was polite with the sales clerk who met them at the front door, but she seemed to ignore everything he said that was not a direct answer to a question. She asked for prices of this brand and model and that, ignoring those listed on the sale flyer, and, when they reached the displays of darkroom equipment, insisted on the clerk checking the back room for recent trade-ins and for scratched or dented equipment which might serve their purposes. Then, having heard all she wanted to know, she began ordering up a squat tower of boxed goods which the clerk stacked on a display case just beside a cash register. Before giving him a look at the cashier's check, the younger barber also asked for a discount for cash.

Within a few minutes the companions were back in the truck with their purchases carefully stored in the bed under a tarp. They got sandwiches from a drive-through window and returned to the highway, counting down the radio buttons to their arrival home. E.Q. breathed more deeply and less frequently as they went west. He began to think how pleased Everett would be to see his fellow tonsorial expert setting up the dark room the next day, finally making Forsythe hers in that way.

✦✦✦

The travelers dropped off their cargo at the shop—Mai now had her own front door key. Tomorrow they would unpack and set up the enlarger, mount the lights, and lay out the chemicals and baths. She realized there would probably be four or five of her new friends trying to crowd into the small water closet to watch and unintentionally interfere with the arranging of equipment they had never seen before and would never bother to learn how to use except to keep her company. She smiled at the thought of their generosity of spirit.

Miriam and E.Q. let her out at the driveway that led to the Thirkell's garage and said their goodbyes for the day. When the truck disappeared around the corner, Mai looked out beyond the property line and to the pasture beyond, so big one couldn't see fence or road as one looked out this way. She set her camera down on the steps to her apartment and walked across the backyard fescue and out onto the unaltered prairie. As she went she picked up a piece of litter, a drive in sack, the only unnatural thing in sight. Tucking the trash into her jacket pocket, she wandered the contour of the land, her eyes following the inside curve of an erosion gully and then a hawk as it hovered in thermal updraft, searching for a place to light.

She began to pick out and identify the different native grasses and other plants—Big Bluestem, Little, Indian Grass, a stand of sumac over where the land fell away. She listened to the sound of the wind as it came around, and she filled her lungs with the stuff of the sprawling sky.

In a few minutes she realized she was getting cold and, thankful that she could return to her own warm, quiet room where she had an interesting book waiting, she turned back to walk home.

Great Plain

In the third inning, Tom "Smoldering" Vitupriano, our third baseman, got into an argument with one of the teenaged umpires about a tag call. I signaled from my spot in the Parkside Min Pins' "dug out" for him to stop, and he saw me from across the field, but he continued.

"I had the ball in my glove when I touched his foot," the kid was saying as I trotted over. Ten-year-old Smoldering had forced his eyes together in a way I knew meant trouble.

"Quiet," the ump said to Tom. "Leave it alone. I've called it."

"But you've called it wrong," Tom continued.

"Hold on, hold on," I said, trying to end the direct confrontation. I went right over to the ump. "What's he complaining about?" I asked in a voice low enough so that the parents in the bleachers couldn't hear me.

"He's arguing about the tag call," the gum chewing ump explained, not looking at Smolder.

"Is he right?" I asked. "Did he have the ball when he made the tag?"

The young ump turned his head and made a face. "He shouldn't be complaining. I made the call I made. That's over."

A couple of the other team's fans were hollering down to us from their bleacher seats. I ignored them, got myself in between Smolder and the ump, and tried to make the best of it.

"O.K.," I said to the ump, but speaking out of the side of my mouth so that Smolder could hear me. "But you understand. He's a bright kid, but he's a kid. He's learning. He doesn't know you have the final say and that he isn't supposed to correct you." Then I lowered my voice even further, intending this only to be heard by the third base umpire: "Besides he thinks being in the right gives him an excuse to be mad."

"I had the ball," Vitupriano yelled.

The ump started to swell visibly. I quickly turned to my player. "You don't say anything. You just play third and leave the arguing to me. Get it? That's my job. Now calm down and go tie your shoe laces."

This last was a code we'd worked out in practice. Smolder frequently got into trouble this way, and I'd told him that when I said "tie your shoe laces," he was near to getting tossed from the game, and that he should retreat and take deep breaths until he felt better. If he spoke again after I gave him the code, he would have to come out of the game right away.

As the ump and I watched in awe-heightened suspense, Vitupriano, red faced and shaking, forced his hands down his sides, took three steps back toward the hole, turned to face the plate, and knelt to fuss with his shoes.

"That's better," said Wally, the ump. "He didn't bite me this time."

We got congratulations from the other team's manager and both umps after the game, especially as Smolder had been hit by a pitch in the last inning and hadn't charged the mound. But the changes in Smolder's deportment were only cosmetic—he still had murder in his heart for the ump and the pitcher, and he was still likely to explode any time.

"Good game, Smo," Jackie Spheris, my assistant, said to the kid as the other players dove for pop in some parent's cooler. "But when you're hit with a pitch, don't rub it."

With the help of one of the parents I managed to get Smolder off of Jackie's leg before he broke the skin. In his teeth the kid pulled away a long oval of Jackie's sweat pants, though.

The next morning at work I heard I was up for a sort of promotion.

Martha, the red-headed secretary who served the office suite I shared with three other museum employees, told me this. She walked into my office about mid-morning, beaming, closed the door behind her, and announced: "Mr. Abbott has you on the Associate Curator's list—you might be getting Emma's job when she retires at the end of the year."

I was surprised. "Really? I haven't applied. I didn't even see job ads."

"Those are coming out right away. But Mr. Abbott isn't going to wait until Mountains and Plains convention—he

18

wants to promote from within, and so he had Barney draw up a short list. And you're on it."

"Wow," I said. And then I couldn't help but ask, "Who else is on the list?"

She made a little face. "Phil."

I shrugged, thanked Martha, and made a show of going back to work. I knew Martha, and most of the long-time employees, disliked Phil, who had a reputation as an "operator" in the museum administration. Phil Durer had too much ambition, it was generally believed. While he had no energy for ordinary civility, he would exert himself to win the promotion. Most of the staff members had been hoping he would find a job elsewhere.

I sat in my office, pleased that at least Martha would rather I had the promotion. I'd thought I'd made myself such a nonentity that no one at the museum would care one way or the other about me. I'd intentionally made myself bland.

This started shortly before I came to work at the museum. Perhaps it is ironic that I took a new job at a history museum just when I had decided to forget the past. I had moved apartments, agreed to help coach a baseball team of fifth graders (how utterly middle American), and traded cars. I had decided to get as far away as I could from the Geoff Urquhart that Janice had broken up with and that had risked his cover to fly back prematurely to the States. New job, new place, new car. New Geoff. And so far as that went, the transformation was fairly easy to make.

I had a little more trouble losing some of my bad habits, and I got back to the fundamentals of the invisible life. I arrived each day at the crumbling Athenian pile before my scheduled work time. I was never fifteen or even five minutes late. And I never took more than sixty minutes for a lunch break, usually staying at my desk to eat salads made up at the grocery story across the street from my apartment. I was on salary, not on a time clock, but I wanted to stop being tardy.

I also reminded myself to keep my eye on the ball, work-wise—I was no longer trying to give the impression of being an ordinary European n'er do well bureaucrat. So whenever I caught myself staring out the window of my little office in the administrative wing of the building, I made myself look down at the vouchers or accession forms laying on my desk, and to get right back to that work. That way no one would pay any attention to me.

Then I started to eat less and to exercise more, hoping to lose some of the fifteen or twenty pounds I'd put on my last few years at the agency. My apartment was close to the museum, only a little more than half a mile away, and so I took to walking to work. I often walked around the western state's capitol grounds outside for a few minutes after finishing lunch.

Soon I felt lighter and healthier. And the Director, Daniels Abbott (his secretary insisted on the "s" at the end of his first name), spoke to me each morning with undiminished cordiality. So even if I didn't have any real friends at the museum, the new me seemed to be working out.

I mused on all of this as I sat silent in my office staring unseeingly at the framed poster that hung on the wall directly across from my desk. It was the only ornament I'd allowed in my work space, something left by the office's former tenant. And now I looked at it. In its central area, with the show's title above and the museum's name and address below, was a fanciful painting of a cowboy riding straight ahead at the viewer. To his right were tumbleweeds and to his left stands of Indian grass. All around was a sky bigger and bluer than anything else. And here the wrangler came, his broad face blank—Great Plain, I'd nicknamed him—but he seemed western because of the chaps and spurs and fringe and rope and all that dangled from him or clung to him as he rode. He wore a large cowboy hat. In only this one respect the cowboy was like me—he had a face broad, blank of countenance. This was my new persona, anyway. Otherwise I was only passing for western, having been born in London—my family emigrated when I was a child, after the horrendous winter of '78-'79.

I returned to my work and didn't leave my office until five o'clock. The doors to the other offices in the suite were open, showing that my colleagues had already gone home. But

Martha was there, sitting at her computer, playing a game of Hearts against virtual opponents.

"I've named them," she explained to me. "The one to my left is 'Daniels,' the one straight across from me is 'Phil,' and the one to my right is 'Geoff.'"

"So how is virtual me doing?" I asked.

"Well, they all behave like their namesakes," Martha explained, seemingly puzzled by my question. "Here: watch a game."

She had the computer shuffle and deal, and she passed all three clubs from her hand. "I'm sending those to Virtual Daniels. It won't do any harm for him to be long in a particular suit."

Virtual me led the two of clubs to start the trick taking. Martha got rid of the ace of diamonds and the others played high cards in suit.

"Looks like Virtual Phil isn't going nello this time," she said. "He likes to overpower the rest of us with long runs and nellos—he goes nello more often than anybody else and usually makes it because we don't remember the option. I'm sort of the distributor in most of these games. Let's try smoke."

She played a low spade. Virtual me had to cover it with the Jack, and Virtual Phil left me a heart.

Two or three tricks later Virtual me still had the lead and couldn't get rid of it. I went back to clubs. Virtual Phil laid another heart on me and Virtual Daniels did the same.

"Just as in life," Martha explained, "Here Daniels likes to go with the flow. He's never so quick with a card as when he's following suit. He piles on."

"But what does Virtual Geoff do?" I asked, deciding to go back to spades one last time.

She hesitated. "I'm not certain I could characterize him," she said. "He never wins, but he doesn't ever reach a hundred first, either." She seemed to sense that this made me unhappy. "I'm sorry," she said.

My lead not only drew out Martha's Queen, but also Virtual Daniels's Ace.

"It isn't that Virtual me can't play." I said, indicating the last trick with a nod of my head.

She shook her head. "I wouldn't think so. But you play everything right by the book. Maybe if you suckered them in occasionally you could catch Virtual Phil over-reaching and put the bitch on him."

The next evening I saw Daniels shopping in the busy produce section of the Mego-market. He was examining the papayas, sliding his palms carefully and slowly along their skin, and then hoisting each one to shake up near his ear.

"Good evening," I said to him.

He winked at me and continued listening to the papaya. "We won't be buying our groceries over the web, will we," he declared, smiling.

I shook my head and began selecting green beans. "You and I won't be," I agreed. And I thought and thought, pretending to examine vegetables. "It may be that the whole web is just for voyeurs," I finally added.

Daniels looked at me as if he were an Anglican priest who had just told a dirty joke. "If only it weren't so cheap," he said, "the legislature might not be so insistent that we devote man hours to running a site, and we could get back to working with real physical objects...artifacts. And books."

"The lazy and the visual are drawn to computers," I suggested.

"Amen," Daniels said. He settled on a papaya or two and pushed his cart over beside mine. Smiling broadly, he asked, "Are you less than enthusiastic about the web?"

I wondered what I should say.

"I've already got an aquarium."

This seemed to amuse him. He chuckled as he walked on out of the section.

The next morning I stopped at a convenience store on the way to work and read the letters in Nugget magazine. That made me just about exactly twenty minutes late. But everybody in my suite came in even later, so I gave up the notion that I should go back to my old ways. If I was going to demonstrate enough personality to win the promotion, I'd have to come up with new quirks. As I puzzled over this, staring un-seeing at Great Plain, I kept thinking of potential quirks as weaknesses. And that gave me a hint. What I needed were some endearing weaknesses that would make me sympathetic. I needed to make myself seem vulnerable. Eureka!

I tried walking around the second floor with my hair mussed, but didn't attract any attention that way. I thought about sobbing in the men's room, but decided that wasn't what I wanted, either. Should I announce I was ill? I'd do almost anything to get that job, but I couldn't think of any good weaknesses that somebody else wasn't already using.

That afternoon Phil was the one making progress toward winning the promotion. Having learned that his name and mine were the only ones on Daniels's short list, he got to work in the handbook. One of his suite mates, Alita Wymer, told me Phil went through all four volumes of the official conduct and hiring guides and then eventually wrote a letter to the Governor's chief-of-staff, who was Phil's wife, as it happens, asking if the state shouldn't have an official policy favoring long time state employees. Alita stole the letter from his e-mail file (his password was "elfagobaco," as apparently everyone in the office knew). In the letter, Phil argued that employee turnover was wasteful, and that draconian political staffing moves should be specifically disallowed by rule. The stop-gap Administrative Order he recommended—and which the governor's office made early the next week— stated that:"Given equality of two applications for a position relative to the advertised standards for qualification and of preference eligibility in accordance with Affirmative Action guidelines, longevity of government employment should be the determining factor in the discrimination among job candidates."

Several days after that order had been issued, Mark Condon, Daniels's Administrative Assistant, called me with the Curator's invitation to an informal meeting about the hiring process. Phil was also invited, Mark told me. Mark didn't like Phil either. "You hear about the new Administrative Order about longevity of government service?" Condon asked me.

"Watch out for that Phil. He'll know that rule as well as if he'd written it himself."

In my mailbox that afternoon there appeared a manilla envelope in which were a couple of photocopies of pages from the Employee Handbook, with specific paragraphs marked for my attention. I thought I recognized Mark's handwriting on the envelope, but I wasn't sure.

Eventually it was time for the informal meeting. We met in the conference room, the only room on our floor big enough for four to inhabit comfortably. But it was big enough for forty. The walls and floor were polished marble. The mahogany table ran about ninety feet long, and the ceiling in the place was so high I could have hit fungos from my seat.

Condon passed the job candidates each a copy of the new museum newsletter, which would be circulated the next day. It noted the organizational attainments and family events of all the institution's employees and was usually headed by an informal note from the Curator, which usually amounted to two or three paragraphs studded with topically unrelated administrative cheers: "Genius doesn't figure when there's simple work to do," was one. "Impossible? Heck, we can't have done half of what we've already accomplished." And sometimes the statements had to do with our specific mission: "Kids love History until adults show no interest in it." I looked over the new newsletter issue as Daniels had Condon read aloud the Assistant Curator job description. The new Curator's letter hinted around about relations with the legislature, reminding employees that the interim committee concerned with web site usage was meeting in town. Another very brief paragraph said we were planning to ask for a large one time addition to our budget for library storage construction. There was also a note saying that Phil and I were the short list candidates for the number two job. The two of us were pictured together just above this entry; Phil was dictating a note into a pocket tape recorder; I was looking straight ahead at the camera, and I was wearing an utterly bland smile. For a second I was surprised to see I wasn't wearing a cowboy hat.

"I have something I feel the hiring committee should be reminded of," said Phil, taking a photocopy from his notebook. "The governor has recently made an Administrative Order concerning longevity of government employment and its significance in promotion decisions." He passed the photocopy to Daniels, who passed it to Condon.

"Yes," said the curator, smiling the same smile I'd worn in the newsletter photo. "That crossed my desk, ah, uh, last week or so."

"I saw it too," I said, introducing myself into the discussion. "But I'm not certain it should be apply here."

Phil raised his eyebrows theatrically. "Not apply?"

I took a couple of photocopies of other photocopies from a pocket inside my jacket. "Well," I said, passing one copy each to the others and still retaining a short stack of papers. "You'll see that Employee Handbook 5.7.38.1947 stipulates that employment by the federal government served immediately before or in the middle of a tenure of state employment shall be counted toward the total for years of service in all state calculations. I worked for the federal government for a number of years before I took my current job, and so it would seem that my years of service should include the total of all that time in my former job. This makes me a fifteen year man, I'm afraid."

Phil, who had worked for the state for thirteen years, stammered. "But that rule was intended to aid returning World War I veterans."

"II," I said, looking at Daniels who was smiling, and at Condon who was grinning behind a file folder. "And that's why I say I don't think the Governor's new pronouncement should be applied here. I believe the committee should set the question of length of service aside."

Daniels nodded once, as if both agreeing and granting me the first palpable touch all at once.

And then I passed out copies of another Handbook rule. "Here's another official dictate that the hiring committee might need to consider. It discusses..." and here I rolled my eyes up and looked away from Phil, "...nepotism. Specifically, the committee may want to examine the passage I've marked to see if all candidates may be ineligible for promotion because of the employment of their spouses or other near kin in state agencies which have some responsibilities for supervision of the museum."

Daniels slapped his thigh and then, afraid of calling attention to himself, bit the insides of his cheeks and began checking the arithmetic in his checkbook register. Condon, smiling, craned his neck to get a better look at Phil's face. Phil studied the photocopy. His mouth was open. I looked to see if he was moving his lips as he read.

"There is also this," I said, producing another photocopy. "Affirmative Action guidelines require that the institution give preference to job candidates who 'are of racially mixed parentage'—my mother is Portuegese and consequently may qualify for the status of 'woman of color' as discussed in 6.18.4b.1982—or 'who represent the recent influx of emigrants.' Have I mentioned that my family came to the United States as refuges?"

"As carpet baggers," Phil muttered.

Condon stood up and began to fiddle with the books and decorative items on a tall cherry wood shelf at the end of the room.

"Very interesting," said the nodding Daniels.

Phil looked flustered. "I'm certain we can get official interpretations of these rules before the committee meets," he said.

Daniels rolled his head. "Please see to that," he said.

Phil gathered his papers and more or less ran from the room.

And Daniels said to me, "Oooo! You play rough. But the quickest wit doesn't always win the fairest lady."

I knew that. In fact, it was my experience that my wit very rarely got any lady at all.

But back to baseball. During Tuesday evening warm-ups, Smolder told me he had to use the toilet. I knew the fellow who ran the Standard station, a fellow who ordinarily didn't like kids coming from the ball diamonds to use his men's room. So I went with my third baseman across the six lanes of fresh black-topped traffic way. I got the key for Smolder, and while he was busy I stayed in the office and listened to a brief description of a difficult muffler job from that afternoon. When the kid returned the key, I thanked our host, and Smolder and I went back to the crosswalk.

A young dark-haired fellow in a khaki jacket arrived at the light just before us, and he immediately pushed the button to get a crossing signal. Smolder and I stepped to the curb and looked both ways. No cars were coming. I wondered why the man who'd pushed the button was still standing there. I checked to see if he was blind and so was waiting for a tone before crossing. But he looked back at me, and then over at the signal.

So I looked again. No cars were approaching from either direction. Smolder stepped off the curb and into the street. I hesitated and then followed him. Smolder stopped once, in the middle of the road, to holler back at the man still waiting there: "Green light, one two three." But the fellow still stood waiting. On the other side my third baseman began signaling the stranger. "Come on, come on," he yelled, waving his arm dramatically.

"Excuse me," I said to Smolder as I walked to the opening in the foul-retaining chain link fence. "Who made you Mogul Emperor?"

"There weren't any cars coming. Why wouldn't he cross? What was wrong with him?" Smolder asked as he trotted to catch up with me.

"I don't know," I admitted. "But you act as if he was hurting you by not taking advantage of the gap in traffic. What do you care?"

We won the game that evening 7 to 4. There were no controversial calls at third, and Smolder hit the first pitch every one of his four trips to the plate. Jackie Spheris patted me on the back without saying anything, and I felt as good as if we'd won a double header.

The interviews for the Assistant Curator job were a week later. Phil went first, and he was in the conference room with the committee a full half hour beyond his scheduled time. But I had anticipated that something like this would happen, and so when he emerged he found me slumped comfortably in a chair, reading Frederick Jackson Turner on western expansion.

Condon was serving cups of coffee when I entered. Besides Daniels, who was enjoying the shortbread, those members of the Board in attendance included Farouk Hasem, Netty Alberry, Dr. Hayes Hume, and little Matilda Warminster (whose family had given the original endowment for the private society).

We soon settled down to business. They asked me what I saw as the future of the institution and what I thought especially qualified me for the position. As I went, I wondered how anyone could be intimidated by this group. Daniels was enthusiastic about any potential tangent that my answers suggested, taking the merest whiff of a new subject from me and then drawing us all off into a few minutes of chatter about how nice the new plantings at the south entrance looked and how true it was that historians and spies were both devoted to detail and how obvious it was that we must make new collections before the artifacts were actually antique, and so on. And the Board members were taking almost all their cues from him. Only Netty Alberry refused to be distracted and kept asking what percentage of the institution's assets should be devoted to getting the web site up and keeping it fresh, and what made me think I would be any good at applying for grants?

I bobbed and weaved and cajoled, never breaking an intellectual or social sweat. And then Netty came to the closer: "I have one last question, and it is one I've already asked Mr. Durer. If you are not offered the Assistant Curator's job on this occasion, is it your intention to stay with the museum, or will you seek another position elsewhere?"

My friends had warned me about this one. They had advised me to say I had enjoyed my time in the museum and would hate to leave it. But that professional alternatives might become known to me, and that I could not in good faith promise that I wouldn't be tempted away from my current assignment.

But I didn't follow their advice. Without really considering the likely reception my answer would receive, I told the panel that I intended to stay with the museum until I retired.

"Even if you didn't get this promotion?" Netty asked.

I knew what I ought to say. But I couldn't make myself say it.

"No," I said. "I intend to serve this institution come what may."

The Board members were silent for several counts after that. Condon gave me a smirk. Then Daniels recovered himself enough that he could make some oblique and apparently unrelated observations about accessioning, and then my interview was at an end.

A few hours later I attended a very different sort of meeting. Suzy O'Lenan, the Parks and Rec. employee who was nominally in charge of our baseball league, had called around to all the managers, and we met, along with a few parents and a representative of the young umpires, in an overheated room at the fire station.

Most of us had just gotten off work and were tired and hungry. And as volunteers, we weren't prepared to inconvenience ourselves in order to attend extraordinary mid-season meetings. So we scooted our folding chairs around the linoleum paved, fluorescent lit, and cinder block walled meeting room, congregating with acquaintances and sharing gunches.

I was sitting with Tim Kuczynski, who whined quietly about how hungry he had become, and Irv Baum, the manager of the Ashton Yard Apes. Eventually Wally the ump came over to sit with us, probably because we were the managers least likely to begin complaining to him about calls or lobbying him with an eye to future advantage.

Suzy came into the room a little late, leading a pair of women she introduced as concerned player's mothers.

"It has come to my office's attention," Suzy said, "That many of the children in the league have begun talking from their fielding positions to the player at bat."

"That's called 'infield chatter,'" Dean McCoverly of the Mount Randall Spelunkers said aloud. "They all do it. Or if they don't, I don't play 'em."

Kuczynski nodded and tightened his belt.

Suzy said, "The outfielders do it too? Then isn't it mis-named? 'Infield Chatter?'"

My back was stiff, and so I knew I needed a walk. I was losing my patience with meetings. Wally said something about consulting the rule book, but that seemed such a waste of time.

"This Enfield Chatter sounds perfectly barbarous," one of the mothers put in. "And sometimes the things they shout can be quite hurtful to the batters."

I wished I had an Enfield rifle about then.

"Its tradition," Big Bearded Bill of the Grocery Clerks put in.

"A tradition like slavery," said one of the mothers, almost under her breath.

"Well, from now on," said Suzy, "Players are not to shout at any player of another team while he is in the batter's box. Wally, please make sure the other officials understand that new rule before the start of play tomorrow night. Are there any questions?"

"I've got one," I wanted to say so badly. I wanted to rise to my feet if only to relieve my aching back. I wanted to say "Does the league exist just to give ten year-olds premature experience at silently accepting the mandates of the incompetent? Or do we have the league so the kids can play ball?" But I remained civilly silent.

Suzy said. "This talking at players who are in the batter's box has gotten unruly and simply must be brought under control. Batters must be allowed to do their best without fear of intimidation. And there must be some regulations or someone will get their feelings hurt." Then she was up and out the door. Meeting over.

Only then could I stand. "Ah, for Christ sake!" I said, tears in my eyes. "Its just a bloody game of rounders after all, idn't it?"

Wally kept the managers in the room after the providers of the new rule had left. He told us not to worry, that those of us actually involved in the running of the games would find some way to slide under this tag.

By the third inning of our next game we pretty much had an understanding about "Infield Chatter." The players in the field simply addressed everything to the pitcher—"No worry, no worry"; "Hum Daddy Hummmmmmmmmm"; "Give 'em the heater; it won't draw a swing"; and such like. Sometimes the players would make up a rhyme or would shout: "Shave 'em!" At that game, I saw one of the complaining mothers from the managers' meeting. She was sitting in the stands eating sunflower seeds and spitting the hulls out. She gave no sign I saw that she was aware we had violated the spirit of the rule change.

Smolder didn't talk it up, but then he never had, even before the imposition of the new prohibition. He stood ready in the field, hands on knees, and stared with intensity at the strike zone. The thing about Smo that had changed was that he hadn't argued with anyone (or bit anyone) since the street crossing episode. Not that he'd become any more social; in fact, he seemed to be more suspicious of me than he'd been since the team's first few practices.

This showed itself in small ways. During the last half of the last inning, we were at bat and Smo had hit a double into the short stop's mid-section and then had taken third on a wild pitch. There were no outs, and the score was tied. I signaled for Smo to wait at third, tagging up and getting ready to run home when Little Trevor hit the ball to the right side. But I noticed Smolder was taking a lead from third. I made the signs again, and Jacky, who was in the third base coach's box, actually told Smo out loud that he was to wait to be knocked in.

But Vitupriano ignored his coaches' instructions. He began to walk down the line just after the pitcher received the ball. He walked farther and farther, all the while turned to look right into the eyes of the pitcher, who blinked, trying to avoid his gaze.

When Smo had walked a third of the distance to home, the other infielders insisted that their pitcher look at the base runner.

He looked. He stood up straight. But he froze when he made full eye contact with Smo, who then turned and ran toward the plate.

Little Trevor, who was watching all of this (as were we all!), took his bat off his shoulder and backed up out of the batter's box.

The catcher stepped forward to block the plate. The pitcher finally threw the ball. And here came Smolder.

He was pumping his arms. His cap flew off. He left his feet, flying head first into the catcher.

The ball struck the catcher in his mask and dribbled away as the impact of player on player knocked him back three feet. And Smolder landed with his chest on home, safe.

Our team ran from the dug out to help him up and crowd around him. I checked on the well-being of the catcher, who was stunned and crying but apparently physically unharmed.

And then I went to congratulate Smo, though I had mixed feelings about his willfully having disregarded my instructions. And I found that he had lost two teeth in the collision.

"You o.k.?" I shouted into the din of my team's celebration. "Shall I take you straight home? or maybe to the hospital?"

His uniform was so dirty one couldn't read the team name on his shirt. And between his remaining teeth and all down his chin there was blood. But Smolder was smiling. "I named myself Great Khan," he told to me.

Phil was named the new Assistant Curator shortly after Emma's retirement party. And within a month or so of that, I was given responsibility for the Museum's web site. My new duties don't fill much of my forty hour work week, I find. So I have time to stare at the picture on the framed poster in my office. And recently I've been considering buying a cowboy hat.

Center For Advanced Thought

As Bridgy said, I'm currently a Fellow at the institution. I'm here, oddly enough, because my books found a popular audience and because—perhaps consequently—my last Dean (there, hanging on the wall) couldn't "find the money" to meet my new salary expectations. A couple of our Fellows are with us because their political party is "out" just now—one will probably get a cabinet seat next time they're "in." One is a retired senator; had he been a lawyer he would have gone to work as a partner in some D.C. firm, lobbying for industry or foreign interests rather than for ideas, which is essentially what most of the Fellows here do. There are over a dozen of us altogether, and three or four appear as experts fairly regularly on the cable television news channels. All the Fellows teach— an occasional seminar, nothing very demanding. And I spend much of my time reading newspapers, supposedly adding to my stock of examples for additional media criticism, which is probably an odd undertaking for a man who had devoted his academic life to the study of Assyrian art, don't you think?

At any rate, I read first of the Wishart business in the *Sun*. Ordinarily I ignore local stories, even about crimes (unless they become causes celeb, like the Simpson murders or the Ramsey one). But I followed this story, perhaps because the first entry referred to an antiquarian book and I am interested in antiquarian books. Then I had my part in the solution of the mystery concerning the crime. Perhaps I should have said in the "solution." And then Meeker himself, who remains a Fellow, used the events of my experience as a metaphor in Congressional testimony, all of which (and a little more) I'll have to recall briefly if I'm to answer your question fully.

Mr. Ian Wishart collected old books, many of them literary and some of them quite old. In his town's small daily paper, he read a classified advertisement for a locally owned copy of the

1686 Gerrard Press *Paradise Lost* and immediately called the telephone number listed there. This was the edition on which Tonson apparently based the correction for his 1688 forth, the edtion also famous for its illustrations. A copy of the Gerrard might turn out to be a bargain, as its sellers didn't know enough to advertise it properly so as to gain the attention of collectors nationwide. Not that Mr. Wishart needed to find a bargain—he could afford to pay a full and fair price.

He spoke over the phone with Mr. X, who was using the name "Laughlin" and who claimed to have found the book among an odd lot of things he inherited from his maternal uncle. Mr. X seemed to know that the book was valuable, but when asked his price, he mentioned a figure little more than Wishart expected to pay for a long weekend's vacation. And then they agreed to meet later that afternoon in the local public library.

Wishart was to have a chance to look over the book or to have an expert look over the book if he liked. Then "Laughlin" would supply a letter and several photocopied documents to serve as a provenance—to prove that he owned the book. And Wishart was to exchange a cashier's check for the volume if everything proved satisfactory. Mr. X said he needed to fly back home, and that this sale would essentially complete the dispersal of the estate's assets.

The offer to let an expert check the book surely comforted Mr. Wishart. He thought himself an expert—and perhaps he was an expert—and he didn't feel he needed additional help given the bargain price. So he had the check cut in his bank and then he drove himself to the meeting.

The Witer Public Library is a museum piece, pretty much unaltered since Mr. Carnegie presented it to the town. At the top of the steps to the front door, Mr. Wishart was met by a leather briefcase-carrying man—five feet ten or so, with dark brown hair and brown eyes, wearing horned rimed glasses and a double breasted navy pea coat—who introduced himself as "Gilbert Laughlin." They went inside the brick building.

Up another flight of steps they turned past the charge desk. "Laughlin" led Wishart around two sets of tall bookshelves, their contents arranged according to the Dewey Decimal system, and to a long oaken library table sitting in an opening in the fiction section under a skylight in the high ceiling. Wishart put on a pair of cotton gloves he had in his jacket pocket. The seller didn't seem to Mr. Wishart to be rushed or anxious. "Laughlin," wearing his own white cotton glove, carefully took the large volume, its binding all intact, out of the briefcase and laid it gently on the table for examination.

Thereafter Mr. Wishart paid little attention to the other man. The book, beautiful in a dignified way, was in excellent condition. Wishart allowed his touch to linger on one illustrated page to feel the paper. It was, as research had suggested, a little more supple stock than that used for the text. He examined the signatures and the sewing (looking especially for reproduction binding or at least for careful mending) and found all to be satisfactory. In fact the book was "like new."

It was also a genuine 1686 Gerrard Press *Paradise Lost*. Only a dozen or so were known to be in existence. This was a hitherto unknown copy.

Or else a stolen copy. How had "Laughlin" or his recently deceased uncle come to possess it?

Wishart asked for the ownership documentation and looked it over even more carefully. The book had been bought by someone named Homer Jaillet from a man named Jedodiah Sly in a northern Virginia town in 1878. Jaillet had given it to his daughter, who sold it to Alfred Laughlin in the early 1930s for $40. A letter on the stationary of a good Baltimore law firm confirmed that Alfred Laughlin had recently died leaving a small pecuniary bequest and some personal property (including the Milton, which was mentioned by name in the letter) to his nephew, Gilbert Laughlin. As Mr. Wishart read the last of this missive, "Laughlin" produced his birth certificate and an Oklahoma driver's license in his name with his picture on it.

"Goodness. That would seem to be everything," Wishart said. "All seems to be in order. If I could just get a photocopy of the birth certificate and the license?"

The other man nodded and handed over a photocopy he had apparently made in preparation for the meeting. Mr. Wishart was already admiring his new acquisition as he handed over the check.

"I hope that's satisfactory," he said.

"It is. Thanks very much," said "Laughlin." "May I escort you to your car?" he asked.

And so they separated. And Wishart returned home to examine the Milton and to re-read the entry in Wiley about this particular rare edition.

So far so good. But that evening Mrs. Wishart came into her husband's study to tell him that an F.B.I. agent was waiting in the foyer to have a word with him. Wishart actually examined the volume again, briefly, because he had no idea why the FBI would be interested in him except because of something having to do with the afternoon's transaction. The Milton was genuine, he was convinced. And so he went to the foyer feeling puzzled rather than fearful.

The man at the entry identified himself as Agent Bagley and showed Mr. Wishart his warrant card. "I understand you have recently met with this man," he said, showing Wishart a poor photo of "Laughlin."

Wishart agreed, led the agent into his study, and closed the door. "I met with him by appointment this afternoon in the local public library," he said, scratching an eyebrow.

The room was dark except for the low intensity light from the lamp trained on the book which lay open on Mr. Wishart's desk.

Bagley cocked his head. "Did he offer to sell you anything? This is a man about whose usual behavior we have some information."

"You mean he sells things regularly? I bought a book from him, a 1686 Milton." He picked up his new acquisition and hugged it to his chest. "You're not going to tell me it isn't genuine, are you?"

Bagley slipped on a cotton glove, held out his hand and accepted the book. "I know very little about old books, sir. But

I have reason to believe it is just what he has represented it to be."

Wishart sighed, relieved. "I thought so. And I did collect documents that showed he had a legal title to the book—a letter from a lawyer, receipts, a narrative of ownership. The book had been in his family." He held up a file folder in which he had put the ownership information.

Bagley, just beyond the throw of the desk lamp's beam, nodded. "Probably most all of that documentation is genuine also," he agreed. "But the man you met with was not Gilbert Laughlin."

Wishart was surprised. "I have a copy of his birth certificate. And of his driver's license, with a photo on it." He tried to give these documents to Bagley.

"Only the license will be a forgery, though we will check everything thoroughly." He took the file folder and its contents. "I have reason to believe that you will be able to retain title to the book—the agency doesn't need it accept as evidence and the Laughlin family is truly extinct. But I will need to have the book and documents analyzed."

"Of course," said Mr. Wishart. "But is this a murder case? Surely the FBI can't be interested in a murder and forgery, can it?"

"At this time we are investigating organized crime and possible corruption of government officials. We will be making the results of our investigations known to the proper state and local authorities, but for now I must ask you to remain silent about this incident. I'll give you a receipt for the book and papers and may call you again if we need further information about the man you met today or if we need assistance in identifying him. Do you understand?"

The agent wrote the receipt at the desk and spilled a card out of his wallet to be left there for Mr. Wishart, who showed him out, all the way protesting his surprise that he should have been even remotely a part of a criminal scheme of any sort.

Wishart didn't hear anything more about his purchase for two weeks. Then he tried the number on the agent's business card. It rang a phone at the FBI's main office, but there was no Agent Bagley working out of that office. There were two F.B.I. agents named Bagley, but one was an older man supervising operations out of the office in Seattle and the other had been assigned to a complex case in Texas, where he had been busy for four months.

The call did rouse interest at the Bureau, where impersonations of agents are never thought inconsequential. Two agents drove out to see Wishart and took down all the information he had about his acquisition and subsequent yielding of the Milton. They also took away the business card and the receipt, and promised to inquire with the Baltimore lawyers' office about the "Laughlin" estate and with Interpol about a possibly stolen 1686 Gerrard Press *Paradise Lost*.

He never heard from them again, either.

I phoned the reporter soon after I read the story, but he wouldn't so much as confirm details that had already been printed. "We don't give out information to just anyone," he told me.

I puzzled over this for a few minutes. And then I called an old friend who works as a wire service re-write man in Kansas City, and an hour later he called back to tell me what he had learned from his call to the *Sun*.

"The local police, who are investigating Wishart's complaint of theft by deception, are getting the dead-fish hand shake from the feds," Big Daddy told me. "The Bureau won't confirm or deny anything, and sometimes they say that this is part of an on-going investigation. The Witer cops think their department may be the feds' target, or that the Maryland state investigation bureau may be. So nothing seems to be going forward, and the man who bought the book doesn't seem to be in a position to demand progress."

"I see," I said. "Did you have any luck with the Oklahoma license bureau?"

He laughed. "No problem there at all. They do have a 'Gilbert Laughlin' on record, a guy supposedly living out in the Otoe nation where they haven't been able to verify the address. But they were curious when I asked about him. So I said he might have sold a stolen antique in Maryland a month ago— no use telling an Okie it was a valuable old book, I figured. The woman on the phone said she'd thought 'Laughlin' was still in jail. But then she checked and discovered he's been out since spring."

"They know the guy?" I asked.

"She called him 'Mr. X,' and told me he is originally from the upper Midwest. Said he works with his half brother, 'Mr. Y.' Apparently they are pretty accomplished bait and switch artists."

"You'd figure the feds would know about this, though, wouldn't you?"

"Maybe not. And I'm pretty sure they don't know 'X' and 'Y' have another half brother who's a bona fide Special Agent."

Thus, "Mr. Z."

"Z's" "Bureau name" was "Armbruster," and as you won't be surprised to hear, there were more than a dozen Agent Armbrusters for the receptionist to search through before she found "Donovan," which was the right Christian name. I decided to play along with what was fast becoming a game and asked her to forward this message (the first secretive-seeming thing I thought of) to him: "They're going to call me Bobby. Ignore Ed." I told her the message was from Gilbert Laughlin and gave her my telephone number at the Center.

"Mr. Z" called me back almost at once. I recognized the authority of the federal agent in his voice. "I'm calling for Gilbert Laughlin," he said. And then there was a silence as he waited for me to commit myself to something.

"Hello, Agent Armbruster," I said. "I'm trying to find a book that I'm afraid one of your brothers may have borrowed from a friend of mine, a Mr. Wishart in Witer, Maryland. It wasn't 'Gilbert Laughlin,' but your other half-brother, or one of your other half-brothers who relieved Mr. Wishart of the book—a valuable old Paradise Lost—in order to have it examined for finger prints. And he seems to have forgotten to return it. Would you mind jogging his memory?"

"I've not identified myself."

"No. I've identified you. But I am only interested in the Wishart book, and not in your identity or your family connections. So, if you wouldn't mind prompting your brother..."

"I have no brother in law enforcement," he said.

"All men are brothers. But I'm also not much interested in your blood relations. May I assume you'll have time to communicate with him by early next week?"

The Wednesday *Sun* carried a story confirming that the book had been returned to Mr. Wishart, rather mysteriously, by the F.B.I. I was surprised. I had expected the brothers to return Wishart's money, assuming they needed the book to continue their business. But then I realized that the book was associated now with "Agent D. Armbruster," and that from the brothers' point of view, later uses of the Milton might lead back all too quickly to "Mr. Z."

That was my part in resolving some of the trouble caused by the crime. I wasn't certain whether my evidence suggested that there was at least one con artist in the FBI or only that one FBI agent probably had two half brothers who were con men and with whom he was in communication. There might have been other brothers, perhaps full brothers, and they might be involved. Or sisters. Or cousins. Or perhaps they had "bent" colleagues to whom they were no kin. Or that folks "X," "Y," and "Z" had never heard of were somehow involved. Anyway I felt I'd been reminded that big institutions are staffed by lots and lots of individuals, some of whom had their own motivations and their own ideas about the ends to which they should devote themselves. I actually already knew this, having learnt it during my days in the university faculty.

At a cocktail party the Center threw for a retired British politician, I told the story I've just told you. Meeker, who is quite gregarious for such an eminent man, joined the little conversation knot where I was telling how a wire service re-write man in Kansas City had used the Oklahoma driver's license agency to force the interruption of an FBI investigation into possible Maryland police corruption all to return to a retired stock broker a copy of *Paradise Lost* which had been printed in 1686.

Meeker listened with a smile on his face, applauded (with the back of one hand striking the palm of the other) when I reached the end, and asked if the story was for general circulation.

"Please don't mention Mr. Wishart's name," I asked him. "And you might want to hide the actual identities of the places and agencies involved. But the story itself you're certainly welcome to."

He thanked me and then used the story the next week while testifying to the Senate Banking Committee. "I have no theoretic reservations about very large federal agencies overseeing American financial institutions. Nor do I object to the tax payers being expected to pay all their agents' salaries. But let me tell you a story to make clear the reasons for my trepidation about the practical ramifications likely if these numerous investigators are not checked by internal oversight."

And then, as you probably already know, he went on to tell about a national investigatory body which had so many secret investigations and so many employees that he wasn't sure whether one or two or three of its operatives (or pairs of operatives) had taken evidence away from a retired Maryland broker. Meeker asserted that the story showed not enough oversight was being exercised. If it were, supervisory personnel at the Bureau would surely have beaten my friend with the AP and I in uncovering the problems. Or perhaps the Bureau's self-policing units had already learned about the possible relationship between the X, Y, and Z clan and the agency. In this case, Meeker suggested that further emphasis on internal policing might have caused the resolution of the broker's problem before it would come to the attention of a Maryland newspaper. Either way, the FBI (like all large government agencies, he implied) needed to be reconfigured.

"Why?" he asked the committee, speaking rhetorically. And then he launched into the so called "Small is Beautiful" speech, so called because of a reference to Schumacker's book of that title. Not that Meeker wanted to make government agencies themselves smaller. Instead he suggested dividing agencies into small parts, each of them with its own self-policing function. The speech eventually led to the formation of the vice president's commission for organizational streamlining which spent several million dollars and produced the one hundred and twenty-seven page flow chart that all the papers have excerpted, usually with much editorial snickering.

Now the last little thing. I was loading groceries into the trunk of my car, which sat in a nearly deserted Humpty Dumpty parking lot, this about ten o'clock one relatively balmy night shortly after the commission began its investigations. A man in a dark suit approached me, stood in the shadow of the trunk lid, and spoke to me by name. It was too dark for me to see his features, unfortunately; I looked, thinking he might be someone I had met somewhere, sometime before, perhaps a former student.

"Do I know you?" I asked.

"You apparently know all about my work," he said. "Otherwise you wouldn't be testifying against my employer."

I was puzzled at first. "Testifying? I haven't ever testified in court."

"This was to a legislative committee," he explained. "You told them we aren't well enough organized. We're getting considerable static because of that." His voice seemed intended to threaten me.

I said, "That wasn't me. That was a man repeating a story he heard me tell at a cocktail party. And I don't think that's what the story proves, anyway."

"Oh no?" he said.

"How could I?" I said. And then I took my Center pass card, a bone-colored plastic rectangle with a holograph and a bar code on it and nothing else, and showed it to the man.

He took it from me and held it to the light. But he didn't seem to know what to say.

"You know, they call me Ed," I said. "Ignore Bobby."

He still didn't speak, but he handed back the card. I turned to lift another sack of canned goods from the cart, and when I turned back to the trunk the man was gone.

Oh, I suppose you might also be interested in knowing about the Wishart family problem, which may be beside the point but which does indicate something associated.

About ten months after the agent took the Milton from him, Mr. Wishart received a check for exactly the amount he had paid for the book—now remember, he had gotten the book back by then. So he had the book and the money. The check was written on a corporation in Delaware which Wishart was soon able to learn was a dummy stand-in for someone or for some extremely well dug-in institution. After using the research department of his old brokerage to trace the ownership of the company back through six other holding companies, he gave up trying to discover who had sent him the money. But he felt uneasy about accepting the payment, so he opened a money market account and deposited the total there, where he could always reimburse the payer.

Then, a month later, he got another check for the same amount from another dummy company. And a month later again. And so on. Some months he received more than one check. Some of the checks were drawn on the accounts of companies from which he had already received checks, or from corporate holding companies he had found in his research of the ownership of the companies which issued the first couple of checks.

He was made miserable by these payments, or so he told me when we talked on the phone shortly before his death—I had called in response to a letter from him written once

Meeker's speech identified me as someone who helped get the Maryland broker's property back. Wishart blamed his ill-health on worry over the checks. "Its raining toads on me," he said.

A lawyer later told me Mr. Wishart's family was at a complete loss to explain the origin of the continuing payments or of the substantial money market account they discovered after his demise.

On his death bed he uttered the phrase, "I do not hate the South, I do not," and the family were trying to figure out what that had to do with the money in the account he had never mentioned to anyone. I wrote them an anonymous note that suggested they give the money to the Witer Public Library in Mr. Wishart's name, and I understand they did just that. But now I've been wondering if I gave the wrong advice: I've read that the library board has decided to replace their building and to add a couple of computer specialists to their staff. All the better to search the World Wide Web, my dear cousin.

To Claim Your Prize

Mary Dexter pretended to be dead. She stopped moving around. She was already pale. And she placed herself where the dead are ordinarily found.

Her grandmother's aging neighbors had been dying two and three at a time, which meant their mature residential neighborhood was increasingly under-occupied. Mary liked that. She preferred the quiet. Mary stayed in the living room where Me-maw had spent her last days rocking.

But after a week the old problem arose. Mary had this sort of appetite. Try as she might, she couldn't deny her interest in the world around her. She knew better. She'd watched daytime t.v., weeping sympathetically, and had read health columns in the paper. But still she found that activity fascinated her.

So she began looking out the window of her grandmother's house. Every day the same menu—dawn; unseen retrieval of newspapers (for study of health columns); postman arrives; ambulance or hearse visits one or two addresses on the block; nightfall; lights on, then off before ten. Mary counted the lights. There were fewer on nearly every day

Catacorner, across a traffic artery (see health columns), a quartet of college undergraduates had moved into the old Turner house. Four young men. Mary got to glancing over there, as there was less and less to see in Grandma's block.

The first couple of days of the fall semester the boys sat out on their porch and watched the college girls walk down the busy street from the sorority houses to the campus and back again. Then, as the trees continued to shed leaves all along the old block, the boys appeared and disappeared. Once two of them came out into the side yard to play what looked like horse shoes. Then there were the scales. Surely the boys put out the scales.

Mary noticed the whiteness because pedestrians kept stopping to look at it. She had to go upstairs to see that it was a bathroom scales there on the sidewalk, north of the house the boys rented and east of Grandma's, across the arterial.

There was a sign taped to the top of the scales, right over the place where you'd put your feet. Passersby looked down at it and read.

Mary wanted to know what it said. On the third evening after the appearance of the white scales, she pulled on a navy cardigan and slipped across the street, unseen and unheard.

The sign said: "We are looking for an ideal person who weighs exactly 128 pounds. Please step up. To claim your prize, if you weigh 128 throw your hands in the air and yell, 'I won, I won, I won.' Thanx. The Mgmt."

Mary slipped back across the street and into grandma's house. But she began to wonder if she didn't weight 128. What did she weigh? She hadn't weighed herself in months. And she wasn't eating much—health columns suggested many many foods are unhealthy

So the next evening she came across the street to weigh herself, confident that she would weigh 128, and yet determined not to throw her hands in the air and yell, "I won, I won, I won."

But when she got across the street, she couldn't find the scales. Instead she found a handful of coins scattered on the walk. She kicked at them, expecting them to be epoxied to the cement, but no.

Furious, she set her jaw and began striding toward the nearby campus bar district. Who the hell thought they could beat her to being the ideal one who was just the perfect weight? Sakes alive, Me-maw would have said.

Pharmacology

Frank doesn't usually like to talk when he's driving. He also doesn't want me to talk. I used to try to read, but reading made me car sick. So now I sit and think as we go. I watch the road signs and billboards, and look at the farms and towns. But mostly I think about this and that.

Not that I always do what Frank wants. Usually I can get him to do whatever I want instead. We knew each other from high school. One of his buddies was my boyfriend. The two of them joined the Navy together. About a year later Frank came home on leave and talked me into marrying him. I started getting most of his pay, so I quit my job and moved away from my mother's.

Eventually Frank found me. I had forgotten to give him my new address. He had quit the service. He got on downtown as a delivery boy for a grill. We moved into his aunt's big white house. And then I got interested in trains.

This is proof that it's me and not Frank who decides things, usually. I got interested in trains, and then he got interested in trains. His aunt had an H.O. set-up on a half-sheet of plywood up on sawhorses in one of her upstairs bedrooms. I got a few new cars and then Frank started hanging around up there with me. He had to run the transformer.

He spent his whole check on more track and started building a little city on another sheet of plywood. He got little trees and buildings and all. Painted in the streets and grass. And then he connected the two track layouts with a couple of bridges.

It was getting hot outside by the time we got the trestles up. It was steaming upstairs, but Frank's aunt didn't own a fan. She didn't want an air conditioner. One night Frank came home from work with a window air conditioner, and she saw him come in. The two of them got into a fight, and he knocked her down and killed her.

So we put in the window unit. After the room cooled down, we brought his aunt in and slid her under the full sheet of plywood.

Next day we put her gray vinyl raincoat on her and drove her into Oklahoma. We stopped the car on a bridge over a lake and got her out. I filled her pockets with bricks. Then Frank said a little something as if we were having a funeral.

"I am afraid I inadvertently caused the untimely demise of this dear, good woman. This fact is especially tragic because of our relationship: she had been my prop and my mentor during most of my childhood, had been the star I steered my moral course by throughout my time in the service of our country, and had contributed substantial pecuniary supplements to my meager salary. Is it any wonder that I adored her?"

"As did I," I said. "But perhaps, given our exposed physical and legal positions, we should move along to a textural sentiment."

"Point well taken, my dear," Frank said. "Ah, Aunt Mary, turn! Turn! Turn! To everything there is a season and a time for every purpose under heaven. A time to live, a time to die. A time to kill, a time to steal. A time to raise up, a time to sink down."

We dumped her into the lake. Then we drove home in time for Frank to go to work. That evening I got to looking through the refrigerator in his aunt's room and found a couple of plastic storage bags full of jewelry.

Then I had this idea. If we took one piece of jewelry a time out of state and sold it, we could buy more train stuff.

And so the next weekend we drove into Ohio and sold an emerald ring to a jeweler at a flea market. Then we bought a Union Pacific set and a sheet of plywood and sawhorse makings. The next Monday, Frank blew his job off.

Every few months we drove off and sold a ring or a broach. We brought more train stuff. Eventually we had to knock down a wall between two bedrooms so that we could have all the track in one room.

Frank's aunt had quit showing up at church. So her church friends called the cops. The cops came to the house several times. They would knock on the front door. When we went down, there would be two of them, wearing brown leather holsters, on the porch. They would ask to see Frank's aunt. We would say she wasn't there. They would ask when she would be there. We would say we didn't know. Sometimes they would come in and walk around the house.

Then Frank started scaring the neighborhood kids. When he saw a group of them inside the back fence after dark, he would jump out of the house yelling. They thought he was a ghost. After that the police quit coming to the house.

I was surprised when Frank began to talk tonight. He was driving us home from selling a small ring. He told me about his duty in the service.

"For a time, I was a Pharmacist's Mate, a modest enough calling, I suppose. One night, as I worked side by side with my superior, filling prescriptions, he told me a little about the nature of his professional training, including a few anecdotes from his days in pharmacy school. The one item of his discourse that I wish to recall here is his claim that there are really fairly few effects one can achieve by giving humans drugs; one can, if I may use his words, 'speed things up, slow 'em down, make 'em swell, reduce the swelling, heat 'em up, and cool 'em down.' Besides the limited ability to localize these effects, which selectivity always involves lesser or greater secondary effects, he asserted drug givers could only claim mixes of those six effects."

"I'd never considered categories of drug effects in that way. Certainly most chili recipes, to offer another example, contain the same few ingredients, variously valued," I added.

When we get home tonight, we will work on the train room. We are knocking out another wall so we can add more track. We toss the hunks of plaster out a back window. Once the plaster is out, we will set up a whole new table of track and run the new Southern Line train. I'd gotten bored with the old set.

The Digital

"I don't know what you mean by Total Harmonic Distortion.
This c.d. player has twelve times Over-sampling."
—a salesman in an electronics store, 1975

I suppose a gauge with a sweep hand would have been more use than the lighted warning on the car's control panel was. When I borrowed Taylor's car to get to work, he warned me that one of those lights was constantly lit.

"Says something like 'Low Traction,'" he told me. "You'll see it. I just ignore the thing. The light's been on for six months. I drove the car to San Antonio and back with that light on. Got the same gas mileage as always. Had plenty of anti-freeze in it, and all the doors were closed and locked. So I just ignore it."

The light remained on all the while as I drove out to the movie theater. On the way I listened to the stock market report, and the Dow Jones Industrials were either way up or way down, I think. Then the newsman read the results of some poll which suggested that residents of our state were more likely to lie to poll takers than were the residents of twenty-three other states. I don't know how they got that from a poll, but then I'm not an expert. When I got to work I went straight to the box office. Jesse was ready to get off when I arrived to replace her.

"We haven't been busy," she told me. "But there have been a lot of phone calls. People call saying they want to see *Jamaica, Queens.*"

Jamaica, Queens was an "independent film" which had been mentioned on television several times over the weekend. The theater chain which owned the theater didn't often schedule indy films, which usually didn't get enough promotion to draw big audiences. So I wasn't surprised that we weren't showing *Jamaica, Queens.* "I wonder why they think they want to see the movie," I said.

"Huh?" asked Jesse. "They heard from t.v. that it was good—five stars. I think that's why they want to see it."

"But t.v. says everything is good," I said.

"Sure," Jesse admitted. "Maybe they want to see it because they figured out that it was about politics and that they agree with what they assume or have heard was the movie's politics."

"Even if that were true, are they actually getting worked up about a movie because of three sentences they heard on television?" I asked her. Before she could answer the phone rang. Jesse and I waved goodbye, and I picked up the phone. "Cineplex," I said.

"Are you showing *Jamaica, Queens*?" the caller asked. "I don't see it in the newspaper ad, and I want to see the movie."

"I'm sorry," I said. "Our regional management..."

"Look, I don't want a lot of excuses. I want to see the movie. It's important. You've got all those screens to show comic book super-heroes and car violence. Well, you need to show an intelligent movie every once in a while. The message of *Jamaica, Queens* may be unpopular, but then that's why the film needs to be shown, to open people's minds. And don't tell me..."

A young couple came to the window. I put down the receiver to sell them a couple of tickets to *Bait and Switch*, a romantic comedy set at a fishing resort. When I picked up the phone, the voice was still going.

"...a well-known fact that the national average..."

I sold tickets to the film about a court case concerning Physics standards on a school's exit exam, *Legal Matter 2*. Then a couple bought tickets to see *Cosigners*, a romantic comedy about a deaf couple, and three young men paid their way in to see a horror movie set at a newspaper, late at night, and called *Printer's Devil*. When I had a chance to pick up the phone again, the caller had hung up. So I put the receiver back on the hook and then the phone rang again. "Cineplex."

"Hey!" said an angry voice. "I want to see *Jamaica, Queens*. What kind of rigged deal is this, your not bringing it to town? Do you know how important it is that the serious cinema be heard, and..."

Then I had more customers. We were running a junior chick flic called *The Plexiglas Slipper* (Cinderella at NASA) and I sold several tickets to that. Two middle-aged couples came in together and bought tickets for *Tepid Springs*, a Civil War romance. When I picked up the phone again, the caller was still going. I managed to be on the line when he ran out of breath. I thanked him for his input and hung up. The phone rang again and I answered. Same sort of call, except the guy kept asking questions. I tried to answer a couple of them before he told me not to interrupt. Then he went on talking and I went back to selling tickets.

That pretty much describes my shift. On my break I went to the office and sat down to read an article in Consumer Reports. I was wanting to buy an electric drill as a birthday gift for my brother, who had just had one go dead on him. But I didn't know anything about drills. I looked at the table of compared features for the twelve models tested and understood almost none of the information there. What were they talking about?

So I asked Max, one of the assistant managers, to look at the table and help me out. He glanced at it. "Oh, just go to Sears and buy a drill."

"But what brand should I get? And what features does it have to have?" I asked.

My supervisor shook his head. "Donny will adjust to the drill he gets." Then Max had an idea. "Make sure it's reversible, so he can take out screws. Otherwise just get the cheap one."

Then I had a couple more hours in the booth. The calls continued. I tried to cut a couple of them short by explaining that I didn't book the movies. But that only seemed to confuse the callers, because apparently they thought I was the voice of the whole theater chain. So when I tried to explain, they got mad. I got to where I wasn't listening to the people who called. One of my customers at the ticket booth was a woman with children who was worried about the ratings. I had to explain the ratings system to her, but I'm not sure I understand it myself. In PG-13 movies there's cursing—"language"—and what they call "brief nudity," but how that's different from what's in R rated movies, I'm not confident I understand.

When it was time for me to get off, I slipped in to see the last reel of *Cuban Heels*, a movie about a touring dance company involved in cigar smuggling. On the drive home I listened to a national sports radio show. The announcers kept interupting themselves to give updates of games that were in the process of being played just then..

When I returned the car, Taylor asked me if the idiot light had been on all the way. I had to admit to him that I hadn't bothered to look at the instrument cluster during the trip home. I mean, I can tell about how fast I'm going by looking out at the world. Don't you think?

Additional Material for Dick Francis's
Dead Cert

Remembering how important appearances could be to people like Kate's aunt and uncle, Alan excused himself to wash up as soon as they returned to the house.

Kate and he had been out for a stroll after luncheon. They had seen her uncles cars in their oversized garage. Uncle Georges automotive collection impressed Alan, the amateur jockey from Zimbabwe. He silently calculated the expense of shipping the vintage Daimler to Africa.

There had been a Mercedes coupe and an old Bugati in the garage, besides three British cars. Uncle George had done well by himself, Alan could see.

Kate had also taken him past the empty stables—her horse was boarded with its trainer, of course. After crossing a paddock Alan and Kate had walked along a stream for nearly an hour. She had talked about her happy childhood, and had not mentioned Dane's recent visit.

When they returned to the house, Alan had seen Kate into the conservatory, an addition at the back of the large brick building. Then he had gone to wash his hands.

The lavatory soap was shaped like a horse, he noticed as he reached for it. Alan rubbed up a lather and then rinsed his hands, but afterwards he could not find a hand towel. There was no towel on the rack beside the sink.

He held up his dripping hands. The room contained no cabinet in which towels might be stored. He considered wiping his hands on his trousers. He considered making use of the curtains.

Then he stepped out into the hallway, his hands still held high. He looked at the wallpaper and the surfaces of an upholstered bench.

As he passed the stairs, he looked at the deep pile of the beige carpet which covered them. He leaned over and wiped his hands on the carpet, first the palms and then the backs of his hands. Then, fully prepared, he could return to take tea with Kate and her Aunt Deb.

To avoid race-going traffic, jockeys with rides in the first two races of a meet generally arrived at the course an hour early. Today the fog had been thick enough that highway traffic was slow and even race trains were running late. The Stewards announced a delay of the first race.

This meant that Alan, Dane, Joe, and Sandy were dressed in the colours of their horses' owners long before the likely new post time. Joe had a pair of dice with him. He suggested a game of craps.

The four of them were kneeling in the changing room when Rupert Grey, a veteran trainer, walked in. He told them to get up off their knees.

He suggested that the game could continue elsewhere. Picking up the dice, he led the jockeys off to a passageway under the grandstand.

He took them to a small, paved area there, out of sight from either end of the passageway. He took a handful of bills from the pocket of his tweed jacket . He asked who had the dice.

Then Grey sank to his knees with the jockeys. Sandy was shooting twenty pounds. His point was six.

A few minutes later, after crapping out, Alan looked around at those gathered there. Joe in purple stripped silks had a series of clear goggles stacked up over the front of his cap. Rupert Grey was blowing on the dice and encouraging the betting.

Dane had on a silver and black blouse. Next to him was Sandy, talking steadily and straightening out the bills in the stack he held in his fist.

Alan stretched and laid down a five pound note. He didn't believe Grey was due a change of luck.

Alan's father sat quietly in his son's hospital room. Alan was still asleep when he arrived, and so he sat down in a chair to read a newspaper and wait.

As he finished with the last section, the other patient stirred on the far side of the room's dividing curtain. A nurse scurried in to check the patient's temperature and blood pressure.

Then a doctor arrived. He nodded to Alan's father as he passed by on his way to talk with the other patient.

After asking about the man's health in a general way, the doctor began to describe the surgery the patient would undergo that morning. He explained that the arteries taking blood from the man's heart had become clogged. The openings were now too narrow to allow a healthy flow, and his heart was working too hard trying to force the blood out the constricted passages.

He explained that new medical techniques made it possible for the surgeons to use a tiny auger, slipped into the arteries, to bore out the channels. This procedure would almost immediately relieve the problem. The doctor was confident of success. He promised the patient would be back at work in a matter of days, and feeling ever so much better.

Then the doctor left the room, nodding again at Alan's father on his way out. The nurse came back into the room to see that the patent behind the curtain took a pill and to attach his i.v.

Then the patient's wife and adult daughter came into the room and went over to speak with him. The patient began to tell them about the new medical procedure the doctor would use on him. To clear arteries near his heart, the doctor would insert a tiny auger into them. This boring out would relieve the restricted blood flow. The man would be back at work in a few days.

The visitors were pleased with this news. But the patient seemed to be getting drowsy. A nurse came into the room and escorted his visitors out.

Once the patient was asleep, he began to talk. He said there was nothing to worry about as this new procedure had been a great success. He explained that the surgeon would slip a miniature auger into the clogged arteries and bore them out. The pressure would then be relieved and the patient would be able to return to work.

Alan's father was still waiting for the nurses to take the mumbling patient away when Alan awakened.

A tremendous wind arose at Ascot on opening day shortly after the first race. It surprised everyone in the stands. Men and women clutched at their hats, some crushing them in the process.

Perhaps because they were larger and more numerous, more ladies' hats seemed to have been separated from their owners. Both those who retained their hats and those who had lost them dashed here and there to retrieve rolling or bounding headgear.

In some cases the hats were trapped against walls, balusters, and fences. Dozens were caught behind the grandstand by a wood and wire fence put up to guide crowds on opening day.

One off-duty stable lad managed to gather up more than two dozen hats, almost all of them flowered ladies' hats. He used bricks pulled from a walkway to hold them down. A steady parade of hat seekers walked by his array of retrievals, and those who found he had secured the hat they sought tipped him.

Kate used a thick ribbon to tie her hat in place. She ran the ribbon up over the hat, pulled tight, and tied a bow under her chin. The hat creased where the ribbon held it, and it conformed to the contour of her head, actually covering one of her ears.

During the third race, one woman's hair came loose with her hat. The wig and several hats blew across the course, causing two horses to bolt. But the shying animals were not favourites, and no horse or jockey was injured when they misbehaved.

Chocolate

Uncle Abner's funeral hadn't much appealed to his chief heir, the relatively conventional Tim Smyth. Abner had long before arranged the whole thing himself, securing permissions and promises. Otherwise the ceremony would never have come off according to plan. Certainly Tim would not have organized the odd service if he had been in charge of the show.

The service was held out of doors behind the local college's chapel. It was a bright early spring day. Unfortunately, the crocuses were not yet up. Dozens of students saw or heard the proceedings as they ambled to or from class, and some decided to audit the goings on.

The coffin lay open on the undertakers' chrome cart, which had been rolled into a bank of irises. Nearby the local Phi Tau Kappa chapter's active membership stood in choral ranks. Accompanied by their lanky Pledge Trainer on the autoharp, they sang "You've Lost That Living Feeling." This idea had occurred to Abner during one of the many early mornings when the inebriated boys had sung loudly from their front porch, just across the street from his bedroom window.

When the state flag was carefully pulled from the coffin and folded for presentation to the local Shriners, one could see that the cat's head logo which appeared on the school's football team's helmets had been embossed in the steel sides of the casket.

Beneath Abner's name on the headstone was carved this simple Latin text:

Veni; Vedi; Venci.

And in place of an eternal flame, a pair of search lights were installed on the vault. The sexton could flip a switch and Uncle Abner's lights would sweep the night sky.

These were the extraordinary details of the funeral and interment. Where Abner had not specified a substitution for ordinary practices the morticians had carried on in their usual ways.

When his uncle's will cleared probate, Tim (who lived in another state) quit his library job. His wife Jennifer sold her share of the travel agency to her partner. And the newly wealthy couple began to garden most of the daylight hours pretty much all day, tilling and training and teasing all of their lot-and-a-half into a beautiful pattern of flowers and well-clipped shrubs. For this pastime they wore thick cotton gloves and knelt on hardened foam pads manufactured for the purpose.

They worked together, usually in silence, accompanied by their spoiled pet doggie, Theodore. They got the hedges trimmed absolutely square by using leveled string guides, planted and charted the placement of bulbs, lined all the flower beds with diagonally set brick, re-painted and re-hung all of the trellises, and rolled their lawn to a satisfactory level. This work was plenty enough to keep them both busy forty hours a week.

Though Tim and Jennifer were in their forties, they had no children. They spoke more frequently to the tubby dachshund than to each other, and they rarely spoke at all with their neighbors, who were busy with jobs and children and such like. One of the neighbors proved to be an embezzler who escaped from his home late one night, climbing out his upstairs window when the police came knocking at the front door.

The quiet Smyths had very quiet tastes after dark and during inclement, non-gardening weather. They each loved chocolate candy, and so they spent most evening hours in their cozy stucco home nibbling bon-bons and then protesting aloud that they were having trouble restraining themselves from eating additional pieces of candy. Theodore would growl and re-settle himself in the wicker bed with red plaid cushion where he lolled each evening away. When he grumbled, either Jennifer or Tim reached out to pat and reassure him. He was always digesting some vast dinner.

As they ate and audibly didn't eat chocolates, the Smyths read novels, usually older books they had checked out from the public library. Romances, they agreed, went well with chocolates. But they both liked adventure stories as well, stories in which ordinary people were accidentally embroiled in some wild conflict between gun-toting villains (who drove hell bent for leather) and the incredulous authorities. Tim would ask Jennifer to put down any book when a scene so gripped her that she began to lean into the characters' car turns or to hold her head or side when a character was wounded in his.

"Jen," Tim would say very quietly. "You're doing *it.*"

Though they were never actually personally wounded while reading thrillers in their comfy living room, the Smyths regularly visited their physician's office. Neither of them was suffering from any major complaint, but they agreed that their good health was due, in part, to their devotion to ritual office-going, daily vitamin taking, and occasional physical examinations. And to devoted study of the health news in the newspaper, which study provided them with material for questions to ask their physicians.

Sometimes they watched the television of an evening, but they were always very careful about what they tuned in. They liked the prime-time feature-story anthology shows, particularly when a story's subject was "Radon: Domestic Killer" or "The New Suburban Assault of Coyotes" or "Mail Fraud Alert!" or such like. "This could happen around here," Jennifer told Tim as they sat sipping herbal tea from the new china cups and watching a story about the havoc wrecked by a slow-moving mass migration of oversized Latin American termites. Tim shook his head in quiet horror. Days when Jen cleaned house, she often left the t.v. on for background noise, sometimes talking back to soap opera characters.

The Smyths always rose to their feet when prayers or the national anthem were telecast on their set (which was thankfully not all that often). And they went to church each Sunday and to the polls whenever there was an election. They voted straight party tickets—Jennifer a Democrat one and her husband a Republican one. And then they came home to pat Theodore and change into their gardening clothes.

It was during March ayear after Abner's funeral, and shortly before their state's presidential preference primary that Tim's nephew came to visit. He was on a business trip, actually working as a political consultant for one of the primary candidates. But as all the decent hotel rooms were booked—no room at the Ramada Inn—the Smyths invited Derrick to stay with them. After all, he had been a charming little five-year-old once. They had a guest bedroom no one had used in quite some time. Derrick had become quite a success during his brief professional career and so it seemed unlikely he would make embarrassing financial requests of them. Besides, he would only be in town for a few days.

"Can't say how much I appreciate your hospitality," Derrick remarked as he brushed his thick and over-long bangs back. "Why don't I treat you to dinner tonight, before I get really involved in the campaign?"

And so the Smyths cleaned their eyeglasses and slipped on their coats.

Derrick eventually picked the restaurant. The natives were unable to recommend anywhere but the chain buffet where they went at noon each Sunday. He said he had an unerring instinct about these things and drove them to Mondo Carne, a steakhouse tucked between a new "suites" hotel and a book-and-compact disk superstore.

"Let's have wine," Derrick suggested. And then he ordered a bottle before his aunt and uncle had a chance to tell him that they didn't ordinarily imbibe. (Tim told Jen, "Scientists have found wine to be healthful," and then he emptied his first glass in chasing his daily baby aspirin.)

"Tell us about your work," Jennifer said to Derrick. "And tell us what you've come to our state to do."

Derrick smiled. "Yes, of course. I take brief contracts to advise political candidates, to write speeches and ads and poll questions for them and to help them influence and react to the press. And I'm here to help Resida Firehurst attract two to three additional votes in each precinct during the primary election next week."

Tim looked puzzled. "I would have thought her politics an anathema to you."

"I'm a mercenary," Derrick said, still smiling. "Republican or Democrat, for or against any issue, my job is to see that my employer's campaign improves. Personally I believe individual politicians rarely attain enough power to be dangerous to us— assuming presidents have the sense to appoint well."

"Isn't it a little late for the Firehurst campaign to be bringing you in?" Jennifer asked.

"I'm a mercenary and a salvage artist," Derrick explained. "I'm called in when hope of a respectable showing is pretty much gone. When polls ten days out show the candidate doing poorly, mine is the phone number politicians call. And because the press also polls and consequently also knows the candidate can't be expected to draw a large percentage of the primary votes, any improvement I can engineer is written up as a victory relative to expectations."

"I see," said Tim. "If Mrs. Firehurst collects twelve percent of the vote instead of the expected seven percent, reporters will think she's done wonderfully."

"And they forget that three weeks ago they were writing that she might finish first among her party's candidates. So if her percentage exceeds expectations, Mrs. Firehurst will undoubtedly enjoy good press for several days in the week of the next primary," Derrick said.

"But how do you improve her results?" Jen asked.

"By doing what her regular campaign staff has been too cautious to do so far." Derrick smiled very brightly at his relations. "I think the secret is to substitute advertising and tactics I actually enjoy for whatever is smart and safe."

Dinner was interrupted by Derrick's pager (which made itself known frequently until he turned it off) and by the importunities of a reporter who recognized the political advisor and interrupted him with questions he smilingly refused to answer. The three Smyths drank two bottles of wine among them—Tim and Jen got just a little tipsy—and

63

the steaks Derrick ordered for them were quite satisfactory. Derrick cut his into very small pieces he seemed to swallow without chewing.

After the meal, he drove his aunt and uncle to the local Firehurst campaign central. The room behind the reception area was a fluorescent-lit expanse of battered desks at which exhausted-looking operatives slumped as they spoke anxiously over telephones.

"People?" Derrick called out as he strode to the center of the phone bank floor. "People?" He smiled and rubbed his hands together confidently. "I have spoken with our candidate. As you know, the most self-satisfied of Mrs. Firehurst's opponents has been whispering that our leader was the unnamed correspondent in two divorce petitions filed in the District of Columbia in the last two years. But what reporters should be asking is why this fellow—for I will not call him a gentleman— has the habit of wearing ties which incorporate gang colors. Sorry to have interrupted your calls. Good evening."

There was a little cheer from the campaign workers, who sat upright in their chairs, and the three Smyths then left the room.

"Will the divorce rumors be the subject of a press release tomorrow?" Tim asked his nephew.

"Unnecessary," said Derrick as they climbed the stairs to his office on the second floor. "Within an hour every political reporter in the state will know about them in a general way and about the gang colors suggestion—we can count on our volunteers to secretly leak it all."

Jennifer took Derrick by the arm. "Who is the opponent making that charge about divorces? I want to make certain we don't vote for him."

"Oh, I made that up," Derrick said. "I made it all up. I'm assuming whichever candidate people think of as 'self-satisfied' will simply give up some votes to Mrs. Firehurst, and that folks hearing that she's rumored to have had affairs will find my rather distant-seeming employer a little more human. Now if you don't mind, I have a couple of other brief duties to accomplish before we go home."

Derrick sat down in his office chair with a plop, pushed aside a stack of magazines, grabbed and used a remote control, and gestured his relations to chairs on the side of the room from which they could see the television screen. Then he dialed his phone as a videotape came on.

Senator Firehurst cares about the elderly and about the children.

A modulated man's voice began as the candidate appeared on the screen, wearing a chartreuse dress with purple piping and with her well-known southern governor's wife hair (poofed up in the crown and with the outside ends making a pronounced flip), surrounded by old folks with walkers and a passel of possibly sedated kindergartners. The smiling Senator bent to shake hands with the drooling extras. Piano music, backed by lush strings, played.

She alone among her party's candidates has introduced legislation to use all of the income from the federal emu tax to save Social Security and to extend pre and post school child care to ten hours a day.

A little boy approached Mrs. Firehurst and took her hands. Then a camera caught his chubby face (which resembled Theodore's, or so the Smyths thought) looking right at the viewer.

"Thank you, Thenator Firehurtht."

he lisped. And then the screen was filled with a shot of her taken from below and with a stiff breeze in her face, two flags (one over each shoulder) flapping wildly. And the narrator's voice read the motto:

Rethida Firehurtht: For the Elderly. For the Children.

as the music swelled. Fade to black.

Examining a photocopied schedule, Derrick spoke into the phone: "Rick? Can you get a decent hairdresser to meet the Senator at Fulsome Crossroads, in Booker County, at nine thirty tomorrow morning. I'll fax you a copy of my plan for the basic change. She can get the haircut in the limo on her way to the Barkers Falls Kiwanis meeting at ten. Important." He hung up.

"We've seen that commercial before," Tim said, and Jen nodded.

Derrick winked and leaned down to tie one of his oxfords. "Do you feel yourselves to be more inclined to vote for the Senator because of what's in the ad?"

They looked back at him, puzzled. "She wants to do things for old people, and for the children," Jen finally replied.

"Yes," Derrick admitted, taking a pair of scissors and a stick of glue from his desk drawer. "But doesn't she look like she might just throw little Hansel into the oven?"

Unconsciously, Tim and Jennifer nodded.

Derrick began cutting details from ads in magazines. "Now here's a picture of Mrs. Firehurst. What would you say if we gave her a new outfit?" he said, and he glued a black dress— shortish and with a minor scoop to the neckline—over the Senator's usual business outfit. "And if we then took a little of the fullness out of her hair..." He got busy with a brush load of white-out.

Jen stared at the picture as if she were Theodore watching the mailman.

Derrick used the remote to rewind the videotape. "And what if this is what the commercial sounded like?" He hit mute and play on the remote and pushed a button on the boom box on his desk, which began to emit the churning instrumental lead-in to Guns and Roses's "Sweet Child o' Mine." Then Derrick himself narrated the commercial.

We look to Resida Firehurst because we know we have troubles.

As the screen showed the Senator reaching out her hand to the kids and old people, Tim and Jen both sat forward a little farther in their chairs.

> She alone understands what we've been through and how we
> can move on, into a new era where life is like a drag of Main the
> night we won the homecoming game. Collect your wagers, and
> take your pick of keggers.

The little boy looked right into the camera and mouthed "Thank you, Thenator Firehurtht." At that moment the music reached full volume and turned its corner into a gritty vocal passage. And then Derrick added:

> Resida Firehurst: Isn't it time we had something to celebrate
> again?

When the tape ended, Jennifer and Tim were nodding along.

"I like all the substitutions," Tim said, eagerly.

"Oh, me too," agreed Jennifer, "unless you think that dress makes her look less dignified."

Derrick smiled. "I think she may have seemed far too dignified up to now. Voters' tastes have changed, and we're simply substituting in a more contemporary political image." Then he asked, "Does she seem, in the second version, to be less for the children and the aged?"

Tim was looking at the new image mock-up Derrick had made with glue and white out. "Who cares?" he answered.

The next few days Derrick was in and out of his aunt and uncle's house. But he always returned at ten o'clock p.m., inquired after their health, and retired "to read a Graham Greene thriller I brought with me." Every morning he was up and showered and dressed and had read three papers before his relations opened their eyes. When they drug themselves from bed at 8:00, they found him in the kitchen cooking breakfast for them from a quantity of groceries he had arranged to have delivered. And as they ate, he tried paragraphs from potential Firehurst speeches and text from upcoming Firehurst ads out on them. And they all enjoyed the week very much indeed. In fact, Jennifer and Tim began to alter their gardening schedules to maximize their time with their visitor. When he wasn't around, things seemed dull.

At breakfast on Wednesday, Derrick said, "Want to hear the new radio spots?" He picked up spattered sheets of handwriting from the counter beside the range. "I've got spots for talk radio and country stations and for 'Mellow Rock' stations."

"No straight rock station ads?" Tim asked.

"Their listeners don't vote," Derrick answered. "Not that they aren't right that way. Here's the one for playing during Mr. Limbaugh's show or for following a medley of Alan Jackson songs. Now imagine the candidate's voice."

> Hello. I'm Resida Firehurst. America faces great moral challenges. The road salt of centralized government is eating away at our national undercoating. Now it's time for us to send the Washington political establishment a message, that we must rinse off before we rust away. That's why I'm running for President. When you vote for me next Tuesday, your demands for a smaller, more accountable government will be heard. And as more and more citizens vote for me, the din will shatter the ear drums of bureaucrats cowering behind locked doors all along the Capitol's corridors of power.

"Now the announcer, a baritone-bass if we can find one," Derrick said.

> Vote for Resida Firehurst, because it isn't too late—yet.

"Yes," said Tim, starring off into space.

"It seems so gloomy," Jennifer remarked.

"Then that's probably the right message for that audience," Derrick explained. "Let me try this other ad out on you. The difference between the 'Mellow Rock' audience and the one for NPR is one college degree, if that helps get you oriented. And again, the Senator's voice begins the ad, but imagine piano music in the background, with strings coming up as the ad goes on.

> Hello. I'm Senator Firehurst asking you, What shall we do with our parents as they grow older? Perhaps I'm more concerned about the future of Social Security than are my opponents in this year's presidential primary because I'm a widow who will

be responsible for the care my mother and father receive when they can no longer do for themselves. Won't you help me to raise important issues—like living assistance for the aged—by voting for me?

"And then the announcer, a soft spoken tenor:"

Resida Firehurst—she needs your help to make government kinder.

"That's better," said Jen.

Tim grimaced.

"I thank you for your help," said Derrick, folding his papers.

Jennifer raised an index finger. "The ad made me wonder about her in-laws, but only fleetingly."

Derrick made a note to himself. "Good. Very interesting. Well. I'm off to the radio station." He stood.

"What's the real truth about the Senator's in-laws?" Tim asked.

Derrick smiled as he took his coat from the closet. "I don't know the answer, I'm afraid. But its too late in the campaign for any answers to hurt us."

Derrick was back to pick up his aunt and uncle about ten that evening. He drove them to the delivery dock at the back of the local newspaper's building and invited them to come along to watch him "place a couple of newspaper ads." They entered through the dock opening.

He gave each of them a computer finger drive to carry and then led them through a darkened warehouse area and up a long hallway with flickering fluorescent lighting, always walking up a gradual incline. At the end of the hallway they emerged into a large open area full of desks, much like the calling studio at the back of Firehurst headquarters except that the desks were all loaded with computers, the screens flickering though the room was nearly deserted. The overhead lighting continued to be dim, with fixtures hanging down low, so that the space above them, all the way to the high ceilings, was impenetrably dark. Offices surrounded the central "bull pen" work area.

Derrick led his party along the side of the room, looking into the opened doors of that side's offices as he went. And then, in one of the offices, he found a young-looking, bespectacled fellow who sat eating a sandwich and fiddling with advertising copy for the next morning's paper, the layout for two pages of which appeared on his computer terminal's screen.

"Hello, Bobby," Derrick said to him. smiling broadly.

The young man immediately stood and his narrow shoulders rose nearer his ears. "Mr. Smyth," he said—while still inhaling—in a light, high voice.

Derrick gestured Jennifer and Tim into the office. "You see, Bobby? I've brought some perfectly respectable subscribers along with me. There's nothing to fear."

Bobby shoved his hands into his pockets. "Oh, I'm not afraid," he said, his voice nearly cracking. "It's just that I haven't handled any of the political accounts up to now. And I'm used to taking mock-ups out to my accounts for their approval or going to their offices to receive camera-ready ads. No one else has ever asked to make up ads here after hours."

"Well, you have nothing to worry about," Derrick told Bobby as he leaned in close to the terminal's screen.

Bobby slipped away from Derrick, and the campaign expert zipped into the desk chair. "That's it," Derrick said, entering a series of commands on the keyboard and watching the results on the screen. "I recognize the software."

He typed half a dozen strokes and asked his uncle for the memory drive he had been carrying. This Derrick slipped into the terminal's USB. Then a few more commands and the copy for a large Firehurst ad appeared on the screen. He then retrieved the layout for the next edition of the paper, scooted along from spread to spread, and finally dropped the Firehurst ad on the back of the first section. "That's what we agreed, wasn't it? But isn't that the ad we ran last Thursday? I think I've got the wrong copy."

"I could check," Bobby said. "The papers from last week are over in editorial. Hold on just a second." He burst out of the office, as if happy for the excuse to go, and began walking toward the far side of the bull pen.

When Jen and Tim looked back at Derrick, he was busy zipping through the morning edition. "Let's do a little layout, shall we?" he said over his shoulder. And they saw he was substituting one ad for another.

"Governor Bannan has made a lot of jokes about how old he is," said Derrick, highlighting the Governor's ad with a swirl of the mouse and the click of a mouse button. "Let's see how readers will like him here." Derrick maneuvered through a few pages of layout and then dropped the Bannan ad in opposite a page of obituaries.

Jennifer giggled.

"He won't like that," Tim said.

"An unhappy coincidence," agreed Derrick, smiling. "But newspapers don't ordinarily guarantee specific placements. We advertisers take what we get. Oh. Look at that picture of a sheep flock." He showed his aunt and uncle the photo at the top of a feature story about predators who prey on farm livestock. "How about this?" The screen was a whir as Derrick lassoed an ad and drug it to the space just to the right of the sheep. The candidate pictured in the ad, millionaire Randall J. Tedesthorne who had an overhanging brow, suddenly seemed to be staring at the flock. The juxtaposition made his mild smile into a smirk, almost a leer.

"And he won't like that, either," Tim said.

Derrick moved the ad which had originally sat opposite the sheep picture into the place the political ad had occupied. "I can think of at least one more," Derrick said as he craned his neck to look out the door for Bobby. Then the political operative returned his attention to the terminal and whir, click, he moved Congressman Chartiers' ad, in color and featuring a tall picture of him with a large American flag as a backdrop. The new home for the ad was in the automotive section of the paper where it was surrounded by dealership ads with their own flags. Immediately Chartier's ad virtually disappeared among the lists of late model, low mileage specials.

"Amazing," Tim said. "I think his ad was made up like a car ad in the first place, but I wouldn't have noticed that ordinarily."

"What are you going to do with your candidate's ad?" Jen asked.

Derrick held up an index finger and then touched the keys. Senator Firehurst's advertisement appeared.

"We're at the back of the first section," Derrick said. "Which is good. But if you'll trade finger drives with me..."

A few minutes later, Bobby came back with a newspaper in his hand. Derrick was changing the font for the new Firehurst ad text.

"Thanks," Derrick said, looking at the old ad on the page Bobby indicated. "I had decided I was reusing the old one and so I replaced it with the new one. What do you say about the copy and layout?"

He rolled the chair away from the terminal to let Bobby, Jennifer, and Tim get a better look.

The ad was topped with a picture of Mrs. Firehurst in her new hairdo. And below that, the ad said:

RESIDA FIREHURST
Your Candidate for President
Promises:
*To keep the public schools open
*To reassure our allies
*To sternly warn the I.R.S.
*To favor the creation of good jobs
*To safeguard our investment in Social Security, despite all opposition
*And to stop pro teams from leaving their native cities.
Isn't it time we all got what we wanted?

Vote for RESIDA FIREHURST
www.Public.Service.zzz

"Oh," said Bobby. "I like the new haircut. Much better."

The three Smyths thanked Bobby and were soon on their way back out of the newsroom.

"I'll bet he'll never notice the ad moving you did," said Jennifer quietly as she looked up past the humming hanging light fixtures to the utter darkness above.

"Who's opposing any action to save Social Security?" Tim asked.

Derrick stopped walking. "You're getting too sophisticated about this business to stand in for average voters anymore," he told his aunt and uncle.

The morning of the election, Derrick began packing shortly after giving Jen and Tim their breakfasts. And then someone rang the doorbell.

When Tim, having pulled his bathrobe tight, opened the front door, there was a tall, sharp featured woman of fifty-five whose hair flipped out at its ends. She waited for him to speak.

"Senator Firehurst," he began, "I'm Timothy Smyth, Derrick's uncle. Won't you come in?"

She followed him into the living room, but before Tim could remove the suspicious Theodore, Derrick stuck his head around the corner and invited the Senator to come up while he completed his preparations for departure. Tim and Jen followed, surprised, as the Chair of the Armed Services Committee walked upstairs to their guest room.

"Are the numbers up?" Derrick asked the senator as he stripped the sheets off the bed.

"Four percent last night. And I seem to be taking votes from Chartier, which doubles the good you've done for my campaign."

She stood just inside the doorway, and Jen and Tim, standing in the hall, peered around her. Jen noticed that much of the fullness of her hair so noticeable in news tape of the early campaign was gone.

"Would you?" Derrick asked, offering her one side of the comforter. They began to fold it. "While I'm on the plane I'll call a couple of reporters I know down south to suggest the words 'whirlwind,' 'sprinter,' and 'fast finish' can be used to explain your better than expected results."

"This has been wonderful," the senator admitted. "You are coming down to re-do the ads for next week?"

"Yes. And I'll fax the new speeches to your h.q. by midnight—should be able to knock those off in the plane."

Derrick looked at his aunt and uncle and smiled. "Here are some people you ought to thank," he told Mrs. Firehurst. "They gave me a stable, domestic context to work out of, the perfect substitute for home."

The senator turned to Jennifer and Tim and daintily offered a large, limp hand to them. "Thanks very much," she said. "If you think of it, you might vote today."

Soon she left to give Derrick a lift to the airport. Derrick took his bed linen and towels to the dirty clothes hamper before leaving. Then he called his aunt and uncle from the plane to again thank them for their hospitality and to invite them to fly at the campaign's expense to the next city where he would be fixing the Firehurst advertising.

Something told them to demure, though. Jen and Tim felt as if they needed a rest after their seven days of peripheral political activity.

And soon they were back to all their old habits. Instead of sneaking into newspaper offices late at night, they read library books. Instead of comparing candidates, they stood for the national anthem. Instead of hearing Derrick's ad ideas and reacting to them, they went gardening all afternoon every day. Back to t.v. viewership. Back to making routine doctors' appointments. Back to Whitman Samplers ("I got the chocolate cream this time and its just too rich, really; I can't have another piece all evening—now remind me").

And then one morning three or four days after Derrick had left, Theodore didn't arise from his wicker bed with the red plaid cushion.

Jen stood in the kitchen and called him. Tim walked cautiously into the living room where the dog lay. "Theo?" Tim called in a soft, frightened voice.

But Theodore did not move. Tim went to pick up the dog, dog basket and all to rush down to the vet's office. But when his hand brushed Theo, Tim knew he was dead.

The Smyths stayed in that day. Late in the afternoon they began calling about their pet's funeral, which they arranged to be held graveside a few days later in the Pup and Pussy Memorial Gardens.

74

Tim and Jen silently cried themselves to sleep that night. Their life's companion was gone!

Derrick flew back to join them for the services, which had been arranged by the pet cemetery manager. The three Smyths, dressed in dark colors despite the warming spring weather, walked along dignified behind the funeary four wheeler, an all terrain vehicle pulling a proportionally correct bier-cart which supported the dark stained little coffin. On the sides of the casket were applied relief depictions of the praying hands and of the flag. All up the rutted "street" they went to the far field, where the fescue had been skimmed off and a deep four by three hole dug out to receive the casket. A soloist employed by the mortuary gave them two strong verses of "I'll Fly Away." And then Tim spoke a few sentiments before the family began their lonely walk back to their car.

They stopped at the back of the veterinary building to see the stone, which had just been delivered. It carried Theodore's name and birth and death dates, and this motto:
Cave Canem
borrowed from a story in a library book. Tim and Jen looked at the stone with some little pride and seemed to take solace from it.

Derrick stayed the night in the guest room and, in the morning, fixed his aunt and uncle breakfast. He told them a little of what was happening with the campaign. But it was obvious those occurrences were of little continuing interest to Jen and Tim. Later that morning, Derrick's uncle drove him to the airport.

"Thanks for coming," Tim said as they shook hands at the gate. "It meant a lot to Jennifer. In fact, it meant a lot to both of us to have the greater family represented."

Derrick nodded and smiled sadly. "It was a very nice service."

Tim made a face and looked off across the concourse. "Yes. I suppose it was. But I was a little nettled when the fellow sang that song. We told them what to have him sing. That song wasn't any favorite of Theo's. Oh, I admit he was one for the traditional hymns. But 'Abide With Me,' more like. Or even

'The Everlasting Arms.' But 'I'll Fly Away,' the man sang. The mortician must have figured Theo for some sort of hick dog. A Baptist. Golly."

Derrick put a hand on Tim's shoulder. "It doesn't matter what anyone thought of him," he said. "Theo's gone on to the only judge who isn't influenced by what's generally believed."

Tim nodded, suddenly sullen. "I know. I know. But you'd think on this one, last occasion the ceremony would reflect the truth about him. And instead they just substitute in something churchy and expect we'll be too unhappy to notice the switch."

Tim and Derrick stood on the concourse, one venting and one trying to comfort. At that moment the airport background music was the churning introduction to "Sweet Child o' Mine," played by a string orchestra. And outside, a small plane arose and turned to ascend with its nose in the breeze.

Ode

I was thinking about how to spend my life when my mother arrived at my apartment on Saturday morning. She told me, "I've been looking forward to this trip all week. All week at work was thinking, 'Once this is over, I can drive into town and enjoy myself.'" "Well, welcome," I said to her. "I'm just in the process of grabbing my turf shoes and heading over to play Frisbee." Then I stood and waited for her reply. She had to formulate her thoughts. "Can I go along and watch? Can I just sit in the car and watch?" she wanted to know. "Sure," I told her.

We took her car. The radio came on when the car started, and I slowly rolled the tuning knob as she drove. She said, "I have the buttons pre-set." I said, "I feel more like browsing at random." 'When we arrived, we picked out a good parking slot for her, facing the field and with the sun behind her. They'd been watering the day before and the "NO PLAY" sign was up. I walked over to where Sean and Riff were sitting on the sidewalk along one side of the field. They were putting on their playing shoes. "'lo fellas," I said. "Beautiful morning going to get hot." Before long we had enough for five to aside. David had the cones in his trunk, and I helped him mark with signal orange the goal lines and the corners of the green field.

While a couple of similarly skilled players divided the bunch of us who'd arrived, I looked to the parking lot for late-comers and saw my mother, sitting in her car. I waved. She waved back.

One day after a game several months before, some of us had gone over to Steve's place to tie dye shirts. That was as close as we would ever come to getting uniforms. A couple of guys had on those shirts the morning I'm describing. The pickers sent them one of the two girls who'd showed up to play and one other guy. That team was the shirts.

I was on the skins, along with Sean, David, Janet, and a fella I had to introduce myself to, our fifth Jim, Combo Jim he became because he played in a small band. Janet didn't need to go without a shirt. Everybody there knew her.

David and I explained some of the conventions of the game to Combo Jim as we went along. "Actually, if you muff a pull-a kick-off throw-the other team gets the disk right there," David told him when Sean dropped the 'bee. "But we've never played that way. Keep your distance, cut to and away from the 'bee, and take your time before throwing it."

"Can you touch a guy when you're guarding him?" Combo Jim asked.

"I don't think you're supposed to," I admitted, "but nobody's going to call hand checking or incidental contact."

"So long as you don't run straight into somebody or hit them with your arm," David added. "Don't hurt anybody. Other than that, everything goes."

We played a dozen points. I was beginning to breathe hard. The guy I was guarding, Jim the Taller, was older and slower than me, and I got behind him a couple of times. But we were standing around too much on offense and bunching up around the 'bee. Their girl, J.R. Salvatori, was real quick. She and Steve broke down the side, trading passes pretty much in stride, a couple of times.

"What's the score?" Combo Jim asked as we straggled back to our goal line in the course of the game.

"We don't keep score," David explained. "Its supposed to be the playing and the society that are of interest to us. Besides, if you keep score, somebody eventually wins."

"It's the process, not the completion," I added.

"Cold pastoral," said David. I chuckled. "It's perfect if it's never over."

Janet, though, was feeling competitive. "She's getting all the way down field on me," she said, referring to J.R. "And then when there's a turnover, I'm alone up field, but you guys don't throw it to me.

"I think I'm looking for skins," apologized David, who was our disk handler.

"I could take off my shirt," Janet said.

"Naw," David said. "No need. I'll look for you."

But a couple of points later, having been loose in the end zone but not having gotten a pass, she did take it off. She didn't have on anything underneath. Janet was nicely formed and all, but not over-endowed, and I guess she didn't hurt herself any more bouncing along without a shirt than she had with one. Two points later I threw her a long one when I saw her unguarded in the end zone.

"That's better," she said, shaking hands with me when I arrived to congratulate her. I looked at her chest a couple of times in the first fifteen minutes after she took off her shirt, and then I forgot all about it. One of the latecomers mentioned her toplessness to me on the sidelines, while I took a breather, a bit later. That was all I heard about it.

After a bit, a policeman came. He parked a couple of spaces down from my mother's car. He watched for a few minutes. Then he got out and stood near one of the cones at the back of the end zone.

"You have reservation for this field?" he asked me after that point.

"Reservation?" I asked. "There isn't anybody else here wanting to play. Excuse me." Then I played another couple of points and found him in the same spot when I returned to the south end zone.

He picked up the cone he stood near. "This says 'Southwestern Bell' on it," he said.

"Yes," I agreed after looking.

"I'll have to take this along and make sure they get it," he said.

"I think it's marking something there," David said as he wandered over. "I think they left it there to mark a line or something."

"I'm taking it along," the policeman said. "And I've had a complaint about your using this field without a reservation."

"Sorry," I told him. "Folks can be real nags, I know." I looked over to my mother, who was watching us very carefully.

"And another thing," the patrolman continued. "That young woman isn't wearing a shirt."

Janet, who had been talking to Combo Jim, turned to look at our little consulting party.

"She's a skin," David explained. "About the cone, officer: if you must take that one along, do you have one in your car we can use to mark this back line?"

"We don't carry pylons," the policeman said, disgruntled. "We don't carry that kind of thing."

"Well," said David, retreating, "then please put that water jug, the yellow one, where the cone was before you go, would you?"

Then we formed up at the goal line and signaled that we were ready for the other team to pull the disk to us. The next time the game took us to that end zone, I noticed that the policeman, the patrol car, and the pylon were gone and that the cooler was marking the line.

It got to be pretty hot out there by the time the rugby boys arrived at about one. David suggested we yield the field to them and walk across the street for something cold to drink. I had been sweating, so I slipped on my shirt and then joined the six or seven others who were crossing to the ice cream shop. I waved good-bye to my mother as I went.

Combo Jim pointed out the "No Shoes/No Shirt/No Service" sign on the shop's door to Janet. She ignored it, walked in, and ordered a green river, borrowing money from Sean to pay for it. The air conditioning wasn't working there, and so once we'd all paid, we went back outside. J.R. and I took off our shirts. And then the whole bunch of us wandered, talking, through the little commercial district thereabouts. Two fellas standing under the theater marquee passed a joint. The bookstore had on a sale. A couple of us jay-walked to watch through the barbershop window as Jim the Rider, an acquaintance of ours, got a haircut.

A guy with a loud car stereo, playing really obnoxious music, went around the block twice. "You know what they say," Sean commented. "The louder the stereo, the bigger the jerk." And as that was my current opinion, I had to agree.

Perkin Warbeck

They were faithful, always clinging to what they knew. They stayed in town when they finished college. They married and stayed married. Though they accumulated fortunes, they continued to dress and think as if they were disenfranchised young people. And they stuck faithful with old friends.

Besides, Wilson, Jill, and P.D. didn't want to lose their poker fourth. As they wandered into their forties, it would be rough to find guys around town who were their age, who liked to play cards regularly, and who weren't any better at it than was Stan Monk.

Another consideration was that he was the guitar player in their garage band, The Backsliders. The four of them were, as musicians, well matched in skill, and Stan at least didn't object to playing the rock songs of their shared adolescence with Wilson (bass), Jill (Hammond organ and Whurlitzer piano), and P.D. (drums), once a week or so.

"Why would you want to leave?" Jill asked Stan as they waited for P.D. to return from the kitchen with cold beer.

"Oh, grow up," Wilson said to Jill. He sat behind an array of chip stacks that had eroded during the evening's play. "He wants to go make some money."

"It isn't that exactly," Stan said. "I'm making enough money here. Not anything like you guys, but enough to support a single man without kids who doesn't have a car jones."

"Then why would you want to leave?" Jill reiterated. "You seem to be doing fine at the college. Old Prof. Carrel's promised to step down as Head and recommend you for the job. You've got poker every other Saturday night, and band practice."

"My wife's offered to introduce you to some women," P.D. said as he handed the beer around. "Maybe Jill's got some likely pals, too, even though she says she doesn't fix anybody up. I promise to go on baiting you about Perkin Warbeck every time we go out chain sawing. You can sit in my sky box at the football games if you want."

"Or in mine," said Jill.

"Or I'll get you opera tickets so you can go with me, like a civilized human being," Wilson said. "And if you don't like your apartment, you can move into my house on the lake until you find something you like better. Rent free. Now, you can't say fairer than that."

"I wouldn't try to," said Stan. "But I've always wanted to have a used bookshop specializing in History, and this is my chance."

"Start one here," P.D. suggested, as if this were a new idea.

"Town's too small. College's too small. But this will work in Madison, and I think I've got the location I want, right across the street from the university campus," Stan said. "Only two storefronts open on the block, and I got the south-facing one. With an apartment over it."

Jill wrinkled her nose. "You're actually going to live over the shop. Hey, cliché."

"You're actually going to move out of state?" Wilson asked.

"I didn't grow up here like you guys," Stan said. "Remember? And I went to graduate school at Cambridge."

"Cut the cards," said P.D. to Jill. "You don't want him starting up on this again. Here we go with this fake scientific crap."

"My thesis," Stan continued, enjoying himself, "was based on my successful attempt to have D.N.A. tests done on the Abbey 'urn bones,' originally collected in the White Tower, under the old south stairway. The tests proved the boys whose bones we tested were very likely related to the Woodvilles and the Yorks—in other words, I proved Richard Crookback had the princes smothered in the Tower. So Perkin Warbeck and Lambert Simnel were simply pretenders. Hear that, initial boy: PRETENDERS, not Richard, Duke of York, grown to manhood in some little East Anglia town."

"Ah, you're just holding up for Henry Tudor, who had about as good a claim to the English throne as Elvis Costello does now," replied P.D.

"Elvis is king. Elvis is king," repeated Jill over and over as she sorted her cards.

"You've admitted not all the bones in the urn are from the supposed two boys, that some are chicken bones and bones from other people and so on," said P.D. to Stan. "Actually your D.N.A. test didn't even show the sex of the original owners of those bones. Or what century they died in. Or whether or not they were murdered. And you don't even know for sure that those are the bones that were taken from the Tower. What happened to the famous shreds of velvet that were supposedly found on the bones when they were discovered?"

"Technicalities," said Stan with a wave of his hand.

"Don't you guys ever tire of that controversy?" Wilson said. "This all happened like five hundred years ago."

"We were History majors," Jill explained to him. "That's how we met."

"That much I understood," Wilson said, frowning at his hand.

"So ante up there, Mr. Romance Languages," said P.D. "You say there's a place vacant across the street from you? Just one?"

The next morning P.D. flew Wilson up to Madison. They were picked up at the airfield by a real estate agent who drove them around and took them to lunch.

The four friends spent most of the Saturday two weeks later packing a rental truck with box after box of Stan's books. After that The Backsliders played a non-paying "Farewell" gig at Bruno's Bar. They began performing to a small audience, mostly of family members and, in a couple of cases, employees. But as the evening wore on they got to rocking, and the crowd grew, first filling all the tables and then packing the dance floor. On and on they played, running right through the break before the last set to work in all the numbers they'd known and loved since they were kids. They left the bandstand laughing, and stood out in the alley behind the bar kidding each other for thirty minutes. The next morning Stan dropped off his key with his landlady and drove north.

The next few weeks were exciting for Stan. He was knocking together book shelves, painting the inside of the store, designing his colophon (actually more of a logo), ordering a sign hung, setting up a web site, joining the district's business association, and sorting out his possessions in the apartment over the shop. He hardly had time to be lonely. Jill called, and P.D. wrote him a letter. Stan didn't get around to even opening his guitar case until he had the store ready to go.

On grand opening day Wilson, P.D., and Jill took out a full-page ad in the Madison paper and in the campus one wishing Stan well in his new business and recommending him to the local consumers of used History books. They also had delivered to the store a big floral horseshoe with a banner on it that said "Congratulations."

Monk's History Used Bookshop got off to a pretty fair start. The first day Stan sold nearly ten percent of the books in stock. On the second he bought two large local collections and began unpacking them, pricing them, and shelving them. At the end of his first week in business and at the end of his first month, he was right about where he'd expected to be, taking in the daily sales he'd projected, collecting e-mail addresses for a regular New Acquisitions electronic newsletter in about the numbers he'd thought he'd get, and doing really better at buying salable books from people just walking in than he had hoped.

Stan had been in business about two weeks when someone took down the "Available" sign from the larger store building across the street. He could see in the two-story high windows, once they removed the craft paper. It was a big space, and with a balcony along one wall, a balcony one reached via a black, ornate circular stairway. Stan walked across the street one day to watch the workmen get the store ready. It was a shop he would have liked to have gotten for his store, but it had been too big and expensive for him.

"Hi," he said to a carpenter who was marking a two by twelve for cutting. "What's going in?"

The man shook his head. "I don't know," he said. "Looks like they've got us making bookshelves, but nobody's told me the sort of business this is going to be."

Stan was interested enough to ask the other area merchants about what sort of business was going in to that attractive space. When he heard it was going to be a bookshop, he wasn't unhappy. Having another bookstore on the block would help his traffic. A used bookshop would be even better for him. If the new store turned out to be a used History book specialist, that might cause problems. But it night simply draw more customers primed for what he had to offer. The neighborhood could become the used History book shop center for the region. Stan was confident he could compete with another store—no one was going to make any money pricing books lower than he did.

But he was startled when he saw the sign painter working on a huge sign for the new store:

Perkin Warbeck
Used Books
Our History is Yours

Stan immediately phoned P.D. "What's with this bookstore?" he asked. "I know it's you, because they painted the sign."

"Did they?" P.D. asked. "Hey Wilson. This is Stanley. They've got the sign painted on the front of the Madison bookstore—no, our bookstore. Stan? How's it look?"

"Pretty good. Thanks for the serifs—I don't think I could have stood having to look at some sort of undignified typeface all day every day."

"Yeah," said P.D. "I stood up for some sort of Roman. Jill wanted puffy bubble lettering like on Free's 'Free at Last' album, remember that? Bill wants every bit of advertising to look like a poster for Jefferson Airplane at Winterland during the summer of love."

"But what are you doing opening a bookstore across the street from mine?" Stan asked.

"Just a thought," said P.D. "Here: Wilson wants to talk."

"Have they got the shelves up? The big velvet curtains?" Wilson wanted to know. "We're going to fly up Saturday, and I want to make sure they've made enough progress so that there's something for us to look at."

"Why are you doing this?" Stan asked.

"Oh," said Wilson, surprised by the question. "We thought we'd try running you out of business. Then you can come back here and we can go back to things the way they were. We could go back to regular poker. And the band could get back together. Jill brought this girl from the college over to jam last Sunday, and that was a disaster. She thought Chrissy Hinds and the Pretenders were ancient history."

On the following Saturday morning, P.D. trotted across the street to bring Stan over for a walk through the new store.

A couple of young people wearing black were shelving books. There were lots of shelves to fill, even up on the balcony. But there were also lots of alcoves with leather upholstered chairs and reading lights and larger spaces here and there.

"What's the steam table for?" Stan asked, dying to look at the books that were going onto the shelves.

"Promotions," explained P.D. "Hey, what would you get for a Folio Suetonius, vf, Graves translation, second printing of the 1990 reissue." He handed his friend a copy of *The Twelve Caesars*.

Stan slipped it from its case. "Whew. I don't know. I'd want to look it up in *The Bookman*. Probably twenty-five."

P.D. nodded. "That's what our manager said."

"So, what are you asking for the book?"

"Oh, $25. But then there's our discount policy."

"What's that?"

Wilson told him, "Half off is you say 'Perkin Warbeck is our rightful king' at the charge desk."

"I can't say that," Stan said.

"We know," said Wilson. "That's the point. We don't want you buying our stock cheap and reselling it for more."

"Well what are you pricing used paperbacks?" Stan asked.

"Half the cover price," said Jill.

"That's what I get," said Stan.

"And then if you say 'Perkin Warbeck is our rightful king,' you get it for one quarter of the cover price."

Stan was dazzled. "So you're going to undercut me on price?"

"That's the idea," said P.D. "And we've got just about everything. I mean, we've made ourselves famous to the book trade in seven states, the last month, offering too much for all sorts of History books. We'll fill this place up and have a warehouse out by the depot to hold all the reinforcements."

"I should be so ticked," Stan said.

"Why?" P.D. said. "Its a compliment, this trying to run you out of business."

The ads for Perkin Warbeck's Grand Opening, ads which appeared in area newspapers all the next week, listed the regular weekly promotions. But Stan got to know them by heart watching them from across the street.

Mondays—five to nine, free Chinese spare ribs buffet
Tuesdays—buy a book, get a tulip bulb—Dutch History day
Wednesdays—five to nine, free cocktails served by peripatetic models, scantily clad, from national men's magazines (soon seconded by former male strippers from a national touring company who served, bare-chested, as bartenders)
Thursdays—live chamber music performances
Fridays—fake pre-Colombian knick-knacks day—one figurine free with each book purchase
Saturdays—book signings by celebrity authors

"Doesn't the barbecue sauce get on the merchandise?" Stan asked P.D. a couple of weeks after Perkin Warbeck's grand opening.

He nodded in irritation. "Our customers are slobs. Luckily that citrus-based detergent cleans just about everything."

Soon bookstore Perkin Warbeck (as opposed to historical personage Perkin Warbeck) got to going. Its promotions and substantial ad budget made it popular and widely known. Actually this didn't hurt Stan's shop, Monk's Used History Books, in the way it was intended. True, PW was selling books cheaper than Stan could afford to sell them. But the two stores didn't offer the same books, or at least not usually. They might each have single volume Herodotuses, but one might have a Modern Library hardback, a Norton, and a Gollancz, while the other might have an Everyman and an Oxford Press. Sometimes

Warbeck's would have the nicer editions. Sometimes their boxed and illustrated hardbacks would go for more, even after the discount, than would the modest editions Stan had sniffed out. Stan's place managed to have more really rare books and perhaps more select antiquarian books than did the newer store.

Some purchasers preferred one shop or the other. Monk's had a couple of regular patrons who bought books from Stan before his closing time every Wednesday and then took him across the street to drink cocktails, free, in PW. In fact, this is how Stan met Cynthia, a former Penthouse Pet who, as a member of the Madison Fold-Out Models Alumnae Association, had on a couple of occasions served free drinks in the store belonging to P.D., Wilson, and Jill. Serving drinks at the bookstore was one of the Association's charity fund raising efforts. Stan asked Cynthia out to dinner.

Then a couple of weeks after the dinner, he took her to the movies, a costume piece about Mr. Moto, operating in the chaos of 1930s Peking. During their post-cinema coffee stop, Stan discovered Cynthia had completed a Master's degree in History at Occidental, writing her thesis about the Popes at Avignon.

One week when P.D. was up for a signing (by Gregory Franzwa of the new edition of *The Oregon Trail Revisited*), he joined Cynthia and Stan for dinner in the Italian restaurant just down three doors from PW.

"Have we about run you out of business yet?" P.D. asked. "I'm getting tired of all this flying, and the Cessna's due for an overhaul."

"Actually," said Stan, justt a bit surprised to be so self-satisfied, "I'm holding my own. Doing just about the business I originally projected. And, then, I hadn't hoped to meet anybody like Cyn. So things look pretty rosy for me right now."

"I don't understand," Cynthia told the old friends, "how the two of you can behave like this to each other, given that one of you is trying to run the other one out of business."

"No malice intended," said P.D.

Stan turned to Cynthia. "They may be a little selfish, but the way they look at this, they're doing it out of friendship."

She shook her head. "I had an old friend try to sue me, once," she said. "Supposedly that was for my good, too. He didn't want me to quit the band and do the photoshoot with *Penthouse*. He said it just wasn't *me*. Also, he didn't think he could find a replacement guitarist in time for a series of jobs he'd just booked."

"You played guitar in a dance band?" Stan asked, wide-eyed.

"Sure. Years ago. Just sort of oldies stuff. Doobies. Savoy Brown."

P.D. was wide-eyed, too. "That's our old repertoire," he said. "Faces? Cream?"

"That's the sort of thing," she admitted. "You remember Mahogany Rush?" Then she asked Stan, "Do you guys play?"

In a few minutes they were in Stan's apartment over his store with the amps on and the axes out, wailing. P.D. rocked out on the conga. Cyn taught them a couple of Punk era songs including the Sex Pistol's "God Save the Queen": "And there's no future in England dreaming!"

The following day, Cynthia took Stan out on her sail boat, out onto Lake Michigan. From the blue sky came a steady breeze that had her tacking along relatively quickly on the way south. But even when they turned for the more direct sail north, still they remained silent, not really pensive but more like sated, every pore full of the experience of a night of music and a following day of leisure cruising as their ears recovered.

"Want to sleep aboard tonight?" she asked him as they approached her usual mooring.

"Got to get back to open the shop tomorrow at ten," he said, apologetically. "If only I didn't have to earn a living, this could all be a lark—snacking over at the Warbeck bookstore and playing music until the early hours of the morning." He slept like a dog that night.

The next day a newspaper reporter came by the shop. Glad to get some free publicity, Stan took her around, trying to show her antiquarian books, good used books, and a few curiosities.

But she seemed more interested in trying to discover: a) who would want to spend any time with History books at all and b) what was going on across the street.

"Over at Perkin Warbeck?" he asked. "I suspect they're setting up for Spare Ribs night. That's every Monday."

"What do they sell over there?" the reporter asked him.

"They sell discount used History books," Stan said, looking out to see what it was that had caught her attention.

The reporter went across the street to ask questions of a young male salesclerk from Minnesota—Eric the Red he was usually called. Then she stayed on to sample the buffet.

The story appeared in the paper on Wednesday. It was all about the quaint trade in used History books. Jill and P.D. were up that Saturday and Stan showed them the story. They, too, were outraged that their retail businesses had seemed "quaint" to the reporter.

"'Quaint' means something like *Strange and old fashioned, but essentially harmless*. Isn't that about it?" Jill asked as P.D. was calling Wilson to tell him about the article.

"I guess so," said Stan. "We could suggest that the same definition applies to newspapers."

"Not quite yet," said P.D., mulling that idea over. "What bothers me is that I've never thought of us as *Harmless*. *Harmless* is about a half step away from *Impotent*."

"They may be said to be the same thing."

"The reporter called you *Impotent*," Jill added. "Me she's pretty much called *Past It*."

The four men considered writing a hot letter to the paper. But Cynthia dropped by and told them the letter would only draw more attention to the assertion that their businesses were *Quaint*.

"Well then how do we make our displeasure known?" P.D. wanted to know.

Cynthia said, "All other things being equal, you could do some damage to the newspaper's business and then tell the publisher why."

"Like start a rival paper?" Jill asked. "No. I know what the newspaper boys are afraid of. Television. Let's get a local t.v. station and use it to scare the paper guys for a little bit."

Revenge kept Wilson, P.D., and Jill occupied for two months. First they had to buy a Madison t.v. station. This involved getting F.C.C. clearance. Then they had to settle on a technique for making the local daily newspaper seem old fashioned and powerless. They inserted a special segment in each evening's newscast called "Science Watch" in which a reporter re-capped a news story about science which had appeared in that day's paper. Then they had on a professor from the university—a different Physicist, Biologist, Botanist, or Chemist almost every night—to contradict the newspaper's story. As the newspaper mostly ran wire service stories, the editors were unprepared to contest the charge that they were printing nonsense about diet, disease, medications, plant life, volcanoes, domestic fowl, the volume of water in its three physical states, and so on. Each broadcast segment ended with the reporter remarking that luckily, no one got their information from newspapers anymore or the country would be in great danger of being misinformed on important topics.

The publisher of the paper, Fritz Shore, eventually called the station. Wilson and P.D. took him to lunch. They discovered they had much in common. He had a Telecast guitar and a Dual Showman stack and liked to play Wilson Picket material. Funky, funky Broadway.

In the meantime, Stan had established himself as the area history bookbuyer most interested, personally, in books offered to him for sale. So the old and weedy Israel Donat brought him three or four books once a month or so, apparently delighted to see the bookshop proprietor wax enthusiastic over rare but not antique biographies of Skanderbeg, Burton, Halley, Montezuma, and Erasmus and dusty tomes considering the political and military adventures of the Borgias, the Hohenzollerns, the Moguls, and the Hans. Stan liked to read these books himself before he put them out for sale. Not that his customers were always anxious to own them.

One month Stan bought a book about Saladin, the great anti-Crusaders general, from Donat and, as it was tulip night at Warbeck, he retired early to his apartment that evening to read this interesting tome. About eleven o'clock he found a series of notes written in a shaky hand in the margins of pages late in the book. Some of what was written was in Arabic. Luckily he could make out the script, and he had an Arabic/English dictionary in his shop. So he translated. Then he got out maps. He didn't sleep that night.

The next morning he called a couple of university professors and asked questions. Then he called P.D. and explained that he had been researching notes found in an obscure book about the Middle Ages in the Middle East.

"You know, when Saladin died, he didn't leave a huge estate the way most of the successful Crusades-era combatants did," Stan explained. "This has puzzled people, because he certainly received gifts and spoils and revenue enough to have been incredibly wealthy."

"I'm with you there," said P.D. "Now I'm pouring my second cup of coffee. What do the notes suggest about Saladin's undiscovered wealth?"

"That it's buried above the second cataract of the Nile, upstream from Wadi Haifa, in the Nubian Desert."

"That's more than a suggestion."

"Oh, yeah. The old fellow who owned this book before me was an Egyptian-American who had visited the site, in the Sudan. He wanted his son to be more serious minded, so he wrote this information in a book he then loaned to his son, shortly before his own death, urging the son to read it," Stan explained.

"Maybe the son did read it and went to collect the treasure," suggested P.D.

"Not much chance," said Stan. "Then he wouldn't have needed the ten bucks he got for selling this book to me. And we would have read news stories about the discovery, illustrated with pictures of the book itself."

"We wouldn't have 'read' about it," P.D. insisted. "We would have 'seen on t.v.' I keep telling you, nobody gets their news from the papers anymore."

P.D. flew up to Madison and studied the notes and maps. He was concerned. "What are we going to do about this?" he asked Stan.

Stan had been thinking over the issue. "Can't really turn the information or the treasure over to the government of The Sudan," he said. "They're into slavery and Christian killing and all sorts of ugly stuff. And they're unlikely to want to preserve the discovery. Remember how the guys in Afghanistan blew up that carved cliff?"

"So we just sit on what we know?" P.D. asked.

"No. Let's go dig it up. The Sudanese are so poorly organized that we ought to be able to bribe some guys into looking the other way while we excavate. Let's just find the thing and carry off a little of the treasure to sell to the British Museum—I know a couple of guys there who control acquisition funds. We can use that money to finance later excavations."

Before they went too far in their planning, P.D. called a U.S. Senator, who was the only guy they knew who had been in The Sudan. "Brownie," as P.D. called him, pointed out that he had only been in the southern end of the country, and that Wadi Haifa was in the north. But he promised to call back after an important vote in the Clock and Watch Face Radiation regulatory sub-committee.

"I'll be free the end of next month for about ten days," Brownie told P.D. and Stan when he got them on the phone an hour later. "I called an attaché I know in Cairo. He's going to dummy up some papers and arrange for us to take a little inspection tour in helicopters. That way we can go into The Sudan under the radar. Literally."

"So, you think the possibility of a significant archeological find sounds like a good bet?" P.D. asked.

"Sounds like a hoot to me," Brownie said. "No red tape, no tours of refuge camps—in, dig, and out. Even if we don't find a thing, it'll be good as a weekend at a golf resort in Ceylon."

Wilson decided to come along when the Saladin story was told to him and to Jill. "I haven't been in Egypt in donkey's years," Wilson said.

"I'm not going," Jill said. "I wish you well, and all, but I haven't got a veil to wear."

P.D., Stan, and Wilson flew to Kennedy and met Brownie. They flew on from there to Cairo. One of the select-a-movies was the old black-and-white *Prince and the Pauper*. When they talked about the film later, it became obvious that Stan didn't know there were separate Alan Hales father and son. Eventually, flight weary, they arrived in Egypt and had lunch at the Intercontinental with Col. "Squeaky" Parsons, the military attaché with whom Brownie had been in Four H—Old Farm Boy Net. Squeaky had a schedule for them.

14:00 to 16:00, nap. 16:00, bathe, dress for sortie, shave, take tea. 17:00, meet transport in hotel lobby.

They took a cab back out to the airport where a Cessna took them south to Aswan. There they checked into the Holiday Inn under aliases. Wilson hired a guide and went looking for Copts. But even he retired early and arose rested and excited.

They boarded a tan helicopter, one of four that went along on the mission. An Egyptian intelligence officer, Lt. Col. Mustafa Hasem, indicated their route on small maps and talked a little about some satellite imaging information Brownie had forwarded to him which seemed to indicate that there had once, long ago been considerable disturbance of the land at the point indicated by the marginalia Stan had found and translated. A nearly round indentation of about thirty yards in diameter remained there. Such a gentle dip in the ground wouldn't be remarked at surface level, the officer explained. But the perimeter was too regular in shape to be natural.

They landed out in the desert two miles short of the border and awaited nightfall. P.D. got up a game of cards to pass the time. Hasem told the Americans he was glad to see they weren't drinking liquor.

Then, an hour after sunset, the noisy choppers started up again. They remained low and kept off their lights. Then, once they were across the border, they skirted the few settled areas and made for their target.

"Be ready to disembark at my command," said Lt. Col. Hasem, translating this into Arabic and repeating it into a microphone so that he could be heard by the armed men on the other helicopters. As soon as the choppers were all on the ground, he barked "Go! Go! Go!" into the mic, and P.D., Stan, Wilson, and Brownie hopped off to follow the Egyptian officer, who went jogging fifty yards south in the waste land, well out of the wind caused by the idling aircraft blades.

"Here," he said, pointing, "I believe you can just see the lip of the indentation."

Men with guns, lights and electronic equipment, and shovels deployed to the right and left. Brownie turned on the metal detector he had brought with him and began to sweep the area inside the shallow crater. Fifteen yards in he signaled for diggers, and three men began working on a rectangular hole.

"This is kind of exciting," P.D. told Stan. "Night patrol archeology."

Before the diggers could tire they hit something hard—a granite sheet. There were inscriptions, which Hasem asked their interpreter to translate and photograph. The men with the shovels began looking for the edge of the sheet.

They found it almost immediately and removed the stones cemented into what was obviously a doorway in the side of the foundation wall which supported the granite. Then Mustafa threw himself down on his belly and shined a flashlight into the opening. He looked up at Brownie. "Eureka," he said quietly.

Each of the Americans took a turn looking in. Stan saw dirty man-made objects—perhaps golden—piled helter skelter to within less than a foot of the granite slab.

"We could find where they buried the masons and slaves who made and filled this warehouse," Mustafa said. "But there is some reason to fear spending too much time on the site. We might draw the attention of locals who might report to their government. Better to grab samples of the contents and escape to return another night."

P.D. and Brownie pulled half a dozen objects from beneath the granite ceiling, stowing them immediately in burlap sacks. Then two men closed the doorway and the shovelers began to fill the hole.

"We'll compact it as best we can," Mustafa explained. "Then we'll fan dirt and gravel onto the site, using the helicopter blades as we ascend."

Their tracks completely covered, the raiding party skedaddled for Egypt. Two days later the Americans (including "Squeaky" Parsons) were sitting in the Cairo Intercontinental examining indifferently made golden vessels that no one else had seen in half a millennium.

"Imagine how much of this stuff may be buried in that cache," Wilson said.   "Well," said Squeaky. "We'll start taking out half a dozen items every month or so. Musty thinks we ought to sell a share to the Egyptian Department of Antiquities. He'll take his cut out of that. Then we'll take a cut to sell outside the country. I believe one of you fellows has a contact with the British Museum who might be interested in purchasing the artifacts—not that I want any of the money."

"O.K.," said Stan. "But how do we get the gold stuff out of Egypt? And no comments about Red Sea parting, eh?"

"The easy way is in a diplomatic pouch. If you guys will trust me with this, I'll see that these first objects are at your hotel in London waiting for you when you arrive there."

"That quick?" P.D. asked.

"It's the real Federal Express," explained Squeaky.

"Then how do we pay you?" Wilson asked.

Brownie winked and got up. "We already talked that over," he explained. "Here's the first payment." From under a bed he pulled a guitar case. Then he put it on the bed and opened it for display. "This is the Les Paul Custom that Marc Bolan wrote 'Bang a Gong' on."

Squeaky was deliriously happy. He took out the guitar, tuned, and played. They began passing the ax around, playing old songs and singing along until finally the desk called and asked them to quieten down.

Stan felt as if he might have oversold his pull with the British Museum employees responsible for Acquisitions. After all, graduate school had been a sort of extended adolescence during which his circle held a drunken salon in The King's Head in the high street on Wednesday evenings after their weekly seminar. Mac and Andre had gone on to gratefully accept jobs with the great London institution, it's true. But this had been years before. Now these guys had faded to become little more than names from his Christmas card list. It seemed likely they would have become formal, reserved, distant, and so lousy with the integrity of this greatest of all museums that they would hardly deign to acknowledge knowing him all those years ago, let alone to make it easy for him to offer them what might be dubious treasures stolen from a foreign country.

When the taxi pulled up at the offices entrance of the B.M., he had to make himself get out. At the porter's booth inside the door he was directed to Mac's office. And when his reluctant feet took him to the correct office door, he was appalled to see that his old school chum was now Assistant Head Curator for Acquisitions.

The secretary, a long woman of sixty, asked Stan's name twice after he told her he had called ahead and was expected, even if he didn't have a proper appointment. "Title?" she asked. He told her "professor" and then was ashamed to have claimed what he had quite intentionally left off being.

There was an exchange of brief messages conveyed over a phone. And then Andre burst in through a side door, his disgraceful tie loose at his neck and his hands stained with ink and what appeared to be paint. He had a plastic bandage stuck to one side of his nose. "Bovril!" he exclaimed.

Stan arose and shook Andre's hand. And then here through the central door came little Mac, slipping on a ratty tweed suit coat. "Bovril! You've come!"

After apparently heart-felt greetings, they retired to Mac's office, which seemed to hold three or four things from every one of the museum's hundreds of collections as well as a bicycle, a basketball goal, and two stuffed dachshunds, their smooth white sides bearing scribbling made by all sorts of ink pens. Stan immediately recognized these as "Autograph Hounds."

"I've got Vincent Price and Buckminster Fuller," Mac announced proudly when he noticed Stan's interest in the dogs. "Here—let's take a look." He lay across a box of ancient scarabs and stretched to reach the larger of the two hounds. As he pointed out favorite signatures ("See—Prince!"), the boys caught up.

Then it was time for Stan to show what he'd brought. He opened the aluminum-sided case and took out two examples of the solid gold artifacts his party had retrieved from The Sudan.

"Here's what I thought might interest you," he said, passing an urn to Mac and something like a gravy boat to Andre. "I couldn't say on the phone, and maybe walls have ears here, but these were snatched from a buried cache in North Africa. There's plenty more where they came from, by the way. And I was led to believe the cache may represent Saladin's savings."

The museum men got busy examining the artifacts. They weighed them, looked at them under magnifying glasses, scraped a little off the underside of the gravy boat for chemical testing, and examined books with lots of pictures (photos and line drawings) of items from historic finds.

"Great stuff, Bovy," Mac finally admitted. "I mean, it's ugly as all get out. But the items are ancient and are ninety-nine and forty-fourths percent pure gold."

"Pretty old for Saladin, though," said Andre. "Oh, I mean, we'll want this lot and whatever else you can bring us from the find. We'll pay, certainly. And thank you very much. But these items may have been made a thousand years before Saladin lived. Perhaps you'll find some bones there or something else biologic we can carbon date. Or maybe the masonry will give us a tip—no photos? I was afraid not."

Stan thought about this. "What would you say if I told you these came from a cache south of the second cataract of the Nile?"

The buyers stared hard as they thought.

"Nubia-way, eh?" Mac said.

"How about old P.J.?" Andre suggested.

Mac cocked his head. "Any Christian symbolism in the decorations? Not that Saladin couldn't have captured all sorts of Christian ornaments. But the big boom news-story about a show featuring these pieces and their mates would say they belonged to Prester John."

Stan rolled his eyes. "I'm not trying to sell you fairy tales," he said. "I'm not pretending this belongs to Prester John or the King of Quivera or O.J.'s Real Killers."

"No, of course not," Mac assured him. "You bring us the goods. We'll figure out how to interest the public in them."

Then they went off to dinner—Chop Suey at a nice restaurant in Russell Square. As their evening of faulty recollections and hearty laughter ended, Stan promised them a regular trickle of new finds from the North African site and gratefully accepted their offer for the items supplied thus far (paid by wire to a numbered account in a bank in the Caymans).

While Wilson, P.D., and Stan had been out of the country, Cynthia had been running Monk's and Jill Perkin Warbeck. The stores were doing the retail business their owners had projected: Stan's was making a three percent return on investment and Perkin Warbeck was losing a couple of thousand dollars a week.

Stan tried returning to work in his own store, but he found the amounts of money that were beginning to pile up in the off-shore account threw off his sense of price. He began over-paying for used books so that two local undergraduates spent two weeks buying books from Perkin Warbeck and then selling them at a handsome profit at Monk's. Not that Stan cared all that much about losing the money. But he was worried that he was only half-heartedly applying himself to the business he had yearned to undertake his entire adult life.

In fact, he was now living off the money from the sale of stolen antiquities, not the mark up on antiquarian books. He wondered what he was *producing* in life.

Figuring to get away and get some perspective, he hired the two undergraduates to run the store through the winter and spring, and he moved out to Cynthia's boat. While he was there, docked for the winter and never very warm, he tried to interest himself in philately. But he couldn't stick it.

Wilson's son Tristen was to graduate from college that spring. Stan, who was Tristen's official godfather, eventually spent some of the money he'd collected from the Cayman Islands account on a new car so that he could drive down to the graduation ceremonies in style.

"What kind of car do you want?" Wilson asked him one day as they spoke over the phone. "What make?"

Stan had never before purchased a car new. "I don't know. Oldsmobile?"

"Good choice. You know this is the last year they're making them."

Eventually Stan bought the cheapest model of Buick and drove it south and west to his old hometown and the nominal seat of his friends, P.D., Jill, and Wilson. He drove P.D. and his wife to the graduation ceremony.

"Nice ride," P.D. told him. "A new car'll make you feel like a million. Does this one have the automatic locks so that the car will lock you out when you're running the engine? I thought so. Progress. You used to be able to take the key out of a running Buick, you know."

At the graduation Stan saw Jill. "Coming back to the bookstore?" she asked. "I got stuck overseeing Perkin Warbeck this winter, and it was pretty lonely up there, let me tell you. And then, the last two months, I had to take over daily management of the television station—Wally the Reed Man suddenly sold all his belongings and moved to the Haight to try to get his head together. Wilson joined the board of the St. Louis Opera Theater, so he's away all the time. And then P.D. is planning a trip to Asia for something or other. You might ask him. Anyway, I'm all alone up there running the Madison outposts of the empire."

P.D. explained his travel project when Stan met him at the reception which Wilson staged at the local hotel. "I'm going to look to see if there are still wild mono-chromatic tulips growing on the northern slopes of the Himalayas," P.D.

explained, leaning his weight against the edge of a long, white linen-covered table onto which waiters were unloading hors d'oeurves. "That's where they originated—tulips. Then the Seljicks brought them to Europe and the Dutch aphids gave them the mosaic virus which made them go multi-colored. One other creep, a Russian, may have actually gotten a little start on me. But this will be the work of months, not hours."

"You were the one who thought Dutch night would pack 'em in at the bookstore?" Stan asked. "Where are you going?"

"Probably into Qinghai and Xinjiang Uygur Zizhiqu—pardon the whistle."

"That sounds like China," said Stan, even more surprised.

"Right," said P.D., sampling the wine. "Its apparently surprisingly easy to sneak into the western provinces. Lots of traders and even some old fashioned caravans go back and forth from, like Kazakhstan and Uzbekistan. But first I have to get to Tashkent, and before I arrive I want to have adopted a Turkmen identity."

"So you're going to learn, what, Tartar?" Stan asked.

"Too tough," said P.D., shaking his head. "Proba'ly Tadnik. I'm stopping in Pakistan to get the language learned and to pick up Islam."

"Naturally," said Stan, his head spinning.

"And to buy some clothes. Want to come along? Explorers and spies, all at once. Imagine the memoirs."

Initial boy was gone for four years. He came back scarred all over his arms, legs and trunk from what he called "little cuts" he took while participating in rituals with "other Sufis."

Meanwhile, Stan closed his shop. He had plenty of money, and more coming in each month through the Cayman pipeline. He tried living in his old hometown, but that didn't work out. Jill was in Madison running what was becoming a chain of local televisions stations. Wilson eventually bought his way onto the board of the Cleveland Symphony, and was busy with that.

When Stan tried to lose himself in college teaching, he found he had as little motivation as he had had to run Monk's Used History Books. Something was wrong. Seeking his roots, he moved to Lincolnshire. He found and let a cottage that one of his forebearers had once lived in. But most of what had been his family's farm land was now owned by a man who was using it as a sanitary landfill. The fellow's name was Terry, and he turned out to be very pleasant. He had a Hofner bass guitar and liked to play 60s Hollies and Animals songs. Terry offered to sell the farm land back to Stan once the landfill space was exhausted. Stan, recognizing a good-will gesture when he heard one, promised to get back to his confrere about the offer. After six months in the old country, though, he felt just as unsettled as before.

Jill's call found him at a motel in Cedar Falls—he had returned to the U.S. and was wandering the Midwest in hopes of recharging his childhood memories. "Can you fly up to do a talking-head shot on a cable news show tonight?" She asked him. "Your segment could originate from our home studio."

"Talking head?" he asked. "What subject?"

"They need somebody with cultural expertise to comment on the crisis in North Africa," she explained. "Actually you'll only have to say maybe five sentences altogether. You won't be the only guest, and they plan for it to be a short segment. After all, their viewers don't much care what happens outside the U.S. unless somebody starts repeatedly claiming the existence of fresh mass graves somewhere."

"That's not my area of expertise—North African culture. I'm more of a Hundred Years War man," he said.

"I'm hip. But they're running out of guys who haven't had their fifteen minutes. And you do know the names of the different countries. So you're way ahead of the other 'experts.' Four hundred bucks and your air fare. Then dinner's on me. What say?"

Stan flew to Madison. Jill picked him up at the air field herself and drove him to the station where he was lightly made-up (by the weather reporter). Technicians put him in a studio and trained lights and one camera on him. Rigging his earpiece and mic was the work of a moment. He was introduced to the interviewers and to the other panelists, all of whom appeared on his monitor. And Jill remained beside the camera as a sort of unnecessary moral support.

Once Stan's "segment" began, he didn't have time to even think. First the other guests made comments about new developments in the news story. They were talking about Islam, and the "anchors" seemed uninformed. Then Morocco was mentioned. "How does Morocco figure in all this, Sam?" the female moderator asked.

"Is it me?" asked Stan. "Well, Morocco is a former French possession, and so it and Algeria are perhaps just a little different from the other nations of the region."

"Really?" asked Anita Krebs, the network personality. "You mean the Moroccans speak *French?*"

Cringing, Stan began by placing Morocco (a map shortly appeared on the screen with Libya, unfortunately, highlighted) and went on to briefly describe its topography. Then there was a commercial break.

"Can you keep this up for a while?" a voice in Stan's earpiece asked. "Congressman Duper hasn't shown up for the next segment."

"I can talk," Stan said. "But I'm not certain I can add anything cogent."

"That's O.K.," said the voice. And then after a pause it added, "And could you please not say 'cogent.'"

When they returned from the commercial, Stan talked a little about Berbers, caravans to Timbuktu, "Moroccan Rock," and the fundamentalist movement. Anita Krebs asked if that was the same Berber as the rugs. In the third segment, Stan found himself giving a seventy-five word introduction to oriental rugs, as Anita egged him on.

"Wonderful," she told him after having thanked him "on-air." "Its amazing how much you know about everything. We must note your agent."

Thus began Stan's new career as "expert in general," known to cable and satellite news channel watchers around the globe. P.D. claimed the regulars in a Samarkand opium den soon knew Stan by sight, though they spoke no English. Called into the nearest t.v. station at a moment's notice, he was expected to enlighten viewers about the Councils of Nicea, the childhood of Karl Marx, Ataturk, Fifth Monarchists, the Portuguese court's time in Brazil, the Fanti Confederation, and basic Hindu pantheism. Much of this he crammed for as international crisis after international crisis required, keeping a copy of the Century Encyclopedia of World History with him always for that purpose. His media employers kept him so busy he had no time to reflect ill on his life, or to listen to old music. Stan told himself that he was finally productive again in the way he had been while teaching college classes—he was a man of *ideas.*

Once, when he was back in Madison to make a convocation address (about the history of poker, oddly enough) Jill took him down to look at the retail spaces where the bookshops had once been. All that remained, really, was a little decaying velvet from Perkin Warbeck's curtains and a bus pan full of rib bones. Stan was getting ready to appear on his fifth show and about his third international crisis of the weekend. "You know," Jill said to him, "you're only pretending to be an expert in everything."

Stan was doing fine until one night when a caller to a program on which he was appearing asked him, "What's new?" He was struck dumb.

The next week he accepted a position, supported by an old endowment, which required him to each week write one editorial (for several ancient Great Plains newspapers) promoting the cause of bi-metalism.

Notes for Jim's Eulogy

After departing from the smoky, pine-paneled restaurant where he was one of our regular Tuesday evening dinner party of college faculty members, the outdoors loving, thirty-five year-old Jim Roper walked across the nearby campus on his way home. It was just after dark. He strolled along enjoying the sound of the leaves in the breeze and the pleasant fullness in his belly.

He stepped into a marked crosswalk on Claflin Road, noticing an on-coming car but assuming he would make the opposite curb before the vehicle's path met his. Unfortunately in this he was wrong.

The Chrysler hit Jim with its right front fender just as he was stepping up onto the grassy parking. The braking car threw him into the air, and he came down on its hood and then onto the broken glass of the headlight that the initial impact had shattered.

As Jim lay there with the wire rim intended to hold one lens bent at a right angle away from his face, his right wrist fractured, and the gash across his eyebrows weeping blood down onto his lap, the driver's side car door open. Footsteps approached Jim and he heard an anxious young voice calling out, "Mr. Roper. Mr. Roper. Are you all right?"

By the light of the remaining headlight, he looked up to see a recent student of his approaching nervously.

"I gave you a B," Jim said to the sophomore. "What do you want?"

Driving Jim to the infirmary, the student bounced the huge car across a pair of flower bed traffic islands, jostling the bashed and broken victim.

One winter, on one of the annual British Theater tours on which we used to lead small parties of students, Jim, Ben Nyberg, and I shared the three twin bedded "Ascot Suite" in a

Paddington district hotel. The room was so small we called it the "Prince Albert in a Can Suite," When a maid took the master key home with her one weekend, we discovered that there was no second key, and we were forced to leave a window open so that Jim could slip in from the outside courtyard and unlock the door whenever we returned to rest and change clothes. Ben, as always whenever he was living in a hotel, had bought some groceries. He stored them in a plastic sack hung out the same window. Jim and Ben both snored very loudly every night.

One evening we were whiling away ten minutes before going out to a play. Ben was shaving in the bathroom with the door open. I was sitting on my bed watching t.v.

Jim began cleaning his glasses. He would take a paper tissue from a pop up box on the night table he shared with Ben, would polish one lens and, after turning the tissue, polish the other.

Then, throwing away the tissue, he would tuck the temple ending hooks behind his ears and settle the nose rests. He would open his eyes, squint, turn toward the ceiling light fixture, squint again, and remove his glasses. Immediately taking another tissue, he would begin polishing with a little more vigor. This business repeated three times.

After the third he was swearing quietly. After the fourth he was clearly furious. This is one of the two or three times I've ever seen him truly angry. Sputtering and red faced, he reached for another tissue.

"Jim," Ben said, leaning in from the bathroom. "I think you'll find those are lotion impregnated tissues."

And so they were.

Jim's friends all know that he frequently gets the urge to be alone with whatever passes for his thoughts. This helps to explain his love of hunting and fishing and his professional preference for jobs he can do all by himself.

During our trips to Britain he felt crowded by the throngs of people in London. He often took late afternoon breaks, hiding out along the river or in other public but underpopulated spots where he had enough uninterrupted solitude to allow him to regain his equanimity.

One year our London hotel was in the Earl's Court district, a blighted neighborhood known mostly as the home of bed and breakfasts catering to Australian visitors, as the address of the annual Boat Show, and as the metropolitan area's dumping ground for stripped cars. Fifteen minutes walk east and south of our towering Ramada was fashionable and relatively secure Chelsea, the neighborhood at the end of the shopping strip patronized by Sloane Park Rangers and other trendy types of sharper edged tastes.

We didn't have group theater tickets for one evening and Jim, tired of the life of London, took off after an early supper to be by himself. He headed toward Kings Road but stopped off along the way to enter a tavern.

The place seemed perfect. It was clean but worn, not sufficiently antiquated in appearance to attract yuppies and yet thoroughly broken-in. No customers sat in the bar. It was quiet there. The bartender drew Jim a pint of Watney's at a fair price and then left him alone. And there was sufficient light so that Jim could write post cards and then work on a couple of journal entries he had been postponing.

In fact, Jim sat immersed in his writing for several hours, ignoring the crowd that eventually filled the place and the attendant smoke and noise. He was writing such entertaining copy that he simply didn't notice anything that was going on around him.

At about nine that the fire alarm went off. Closing his journal he stood, looking for smoke or flames, and joined the other patrons in making for the door.

As they filed out he realized that the other customers were all men. And that they were all wearing odd leather garments—service caps, motorcycle chaps, vests (without shirts underneath), and halter boots.

He had spent the evening in a leather bar for homosexuals, and he claims he was repeatedly pinched on the behind as he tried to navigate between the other ejected customers who waited on the sidewalk for the alarm to be turned off.

He offered to show some of us the black and blue marks the pinches had caused, but we refused the viewing opportunity. Jim's lack of ordinary modesty seems as inordinate as is his desire for privacy.

After the leather bar evening, Jim decided to change his practice and take his private hours in outdoors public spaces. But he was propositioned twice in half an hour the next evening in Green Park, so he resigned himself to the company of the other members of the university party, and he would simply ignore us for a couple of hours every day until our itinerary took us to Bath where he could again roam free and alone without fear of suffering welts.

Inspired by an episode of the old Perry Mason television series, I once sent Jim an anonymous letter. I cut out words and letters from the newspaper and pasted them to a sheet of typing bond so that they read:

Mr. Roper
We know what you have buried in your garden. Beware, beware, for the wheels of justice grind slow but fine.

And then, using an old manual typewriter, I put his home address on a plain envelope and sent the message off.

Several days later, Jim called. "I just got the oddest letter," he said, sounding wary. "I don't know what to make of it. Probably the neighbor boys sent it."

I asked. "Was it sent anonymously?"

"Yes," he said, "And it's made up of words cut from the newspaper."

I chuckled. "Sounds like a joke."

"Could be," he agreed. "But here's the message." He read it to me.

I laughed aloud. "Somebody's kidding you. Or do you have something buried in your garden?"

"Not that I know of," he said.

This was the last I heard about the letter for a couple of days. Then he called to say a friend of ours who is a policeman had dropped by the house for a chat and had found the letter open on the coffee table.

"Les thought it was pretty interesting," Jim told me. "He said he'd take it down to the station and ask other officers to see if anyone else had heard of prank letters like that one being received around town."

Two weeks later I was riding my bike up Jarvis Drive and saw a yellow backhoe being unloaded into Jim's driveway. I put my Raleigh on its kickstand and went up to ask about the arrival of the heavy equipment.

Jim was inside brewing tea. "I didn't order it," he said, referring to the earth mover. "The K.B.I. did."

"The K.B.I.?" I asked, surprised.

"They eventually got ahold of the anonymous note," Jim explained.

Inside a running fence of yellow "Crime Scene, Do Not Enter" plastic tape, the backhoe dug up much of Jim's backyard. Bones buried there by dogs and rusting construction debris were sifted out and taken to Topeka where forensic scientists were to "interpret" them.

As Jim told me later, "I figured the note was a joke, but the law enforcement boys all enjoyed the business so much. They loved anticipating and planning the excavation and got so much joy out of working outside that they didn't seem all that disappointed when they didn't find anything odd in the carrot and radish beds."

Jim did not, to my knowledge, receive a final official report on the evidence.

I once called "Hunter Jim" away from work on the carcass of a deer he had shot. He was scraping the hide for tanning, having earlier butchered the meat and wrapped it for freezing. He does the butchering in the garage because of all the mess of blood and offal.

I called that night because just before supper I had cut the back of my upper arm with a pane of glass I was replacing in one of our front porch windows. After cleaning the wound and bandaging it, I had gone on with my routine for the remainder of the evening, expecting the bleeding to stop.

Letterman was on when I gave up that notion and called Jim to ask him to take me to the emergency room at Memorial Hospital. He washed his hands and drove by to pick me up.

At the hospital, the crew was sympathetic enough, especially as Jim and I were joking about the nature and cause of my injury. The nurse and doctor had me sit on a paper-covered roller bed after they had heard my apology for giving them unnecessary work.

"No," said the young doctor. "You were right to come in. The puncture isn't broad, but it is deep, and it wouldn't close up over the short haul without a little help. See?" he said, turning my arm slightly so that the nurse could take a look.

"Oh, yeah," she said. Then she stepped out of the way and held the arm out for Roper to examine. "See?" she asked him.

He fainted dead away onto a chair.

I helped pick him up and put him on the roller bed. The medicos worked over him for a few minutes, checking his pulse and respiration, patting his cheeks, and even unbuttoning his deer blood-smeared flannel shirt. After consulting informally with the doctor, the nurse went to get the apparatus for giving Jim oxygen through a mask. When he was comfortable and had regained consciousness, the doctor took me into another stall and stitched me up, taking only a couple of minutes to do that and to give me a tetanus shot before crossing back over to attend to Jim.

I went over to speak with him after half an hour. An hour and a half after he fainted, they let him up. The staff helped Jim into a wheelchair to get him out to the car. Then I drove him home and helped him up onto the porch, opened the door with his key, and took his shoes off for him as he lay on his bed. After saying hello to his nephew, who was still working on the deer hide in the garage, I walked home.

I understand the follow-up examination found Jim to be generally healthy.

A year later, when another doctor discovered the "hot nodule" on Jim's thyroid gland, that explained my friend's lack of vigor and so, in a way, we were relieved. When the patient started to hear some of the details associated with the planned treatment, he began to make jokes.

The radioactive power of the iodine dose he was to receive in Topeka was so strong that the Nuclear Regulatory Commission, Jim was told, had to authorize its issuance. He was instructed to flush the toilet twice after each use, once he had taken the Geiger Counter-prompting dose, to scrub the bathtub after each bath, and to avoid kissing anyone on the mouth ("As if," he said to me when he related this temporary rule for his deportment). Jim asked if he would, after swallowing the dose, be visible in the dark to the naked eye, but the doctor didn't seem to understand the question.

Jim decided to turn his treatment into a business opportunity. He advertised pints of radioactive urine for home gardeners. He called a local television dealer, offering to stand just outside the showroom of a competitor on a busy Saturday in order to goof up broadcast reception. And he wrote Western Resources with a low bid for repainting the nuclear reactor at Wolf Creek (figuring to do that instead of taking the iodine, thus lowering his medical costs).

Contacting students in university chemistry classes, he suggested that for a small fee he could unobtrusively invalidate the results of test experiments their professors were staging. He threatened to call a favorite local truck farmer to say he'd come out and irradiate her tomatoes in a swap for fresh broccoli.

But none of these business offerings were accepted. Oh, he sold a few pints of urine, but I'm not certain who bought them or to what use they put them.

For years Jim and I have been driving down to Hutchinson to watch the first day of the National Junior College Men's Basketball Tournament, six games played with shortened halftimes and limited time outs in the old aircraft hanger of a field house there, its lighting far too dim and its floor yellowing more and more as the seasons of unstripped waxing pass.

I think it's fair to say we are attracted more by the ritual than by the sport. One or the other of us drives and we meet my father, arriving from Winfield, at the News where we buy tourney editions. Then we go to a diner that was once called Deak's, then Chelsea's, where we always eat about the same thing. Jim likes the b.l.t., I think.

We always see at least part of all six afternoon halves of no-defense, highly athletic basketball. We repeat all the ritual jokes about the working class crowd, the squirrely looking little cheerleaders (and, attendant on most of the squads, the two dorky looking guy yell leaders who wear double knit shorts and wield megaphones), about the ridiculously amateur mascots (some short and "peppy" persons costumed in team-color sweats and with papier mache heads of some sort), about the dependable rotation of local high school stage bands and junior high drill teams as intermission entertainers, and about the wildly unpredictable quality of the invocation. During the halftimes and between games we wander the smoky concourse, picking out famous and would-be-famous division one coaches who are there to watch potential recruits.

Around five we drive out to the Airport Steakhouse for the comfortably conventional dinners and more rubbernecking. Pop leaves the Sports Arena after the first of the three evening games. Jim and I usually try to see at least a little of even the last offering. Sometimes something noteworthy happens on court—Nolan Richardson appears in the coach's box in a rented dinner jacket, say, or five foot four inch Spud Webb suddenly drives to the basket and dunks the ball. Generally speaking, though, by the fourth game the teams have begun to blur together and by the sixth one can barely force oneself to focus on the play. When we can hardly hold our heads up, we drive home. One year Jim took us on a sixty mile an hour slide as we rotated three hundred and sixty degrees in our orientation to the highway just west of Inman, but usually we make it home without anything much having happened really all day.

The most memorable moment of all of these trips occurred as we were driving out I70 on our way to Hutch one still-frosty March, relaxed and anticipating a satisfactory day of sort of watching basketball. We had just passed Enterprise and had seen a big flock of wild turkeys walking in a line along a windbreak in a winter wheat field when Jim popped the traveling tape he'd made the night before into the cassette player. It was something neither of us had heard for years, The Supremes' Greatest Hits. About the first chorus of "Baby Love," we had to pull over and get out of the car and walk, hooting, down the shoulder of the Interstate, we were so overcome by delight, Jim arching his neck and calling out.

Jim has always been very fond of music, and he has always liked buy things through the mail. He gets clothes from Cabella's sale catalogs and fishing gear from addresses advertised in Field and Stream . Somehow he got on the mailing list of an outfit which sells pre-mixed seasoning for deer hunters to use in making sausage of their kill. This year Jim got two does and turned them into all sorts of sausage—andoule, chirizo, and something I think he called "English Breakfast Sausage," the thought of which makes me more than a little wambly. Altogether he made something like 120 pounds of sausage from this year's venison.

"I'll have to buy a chicken every week," he confessed. "A diet of nothing but sausage gets a little monotonous."

I asked if he had any sausage left after last year. After pausing to think, he answered, "About forty pounds."

Over the last few years, record companies have sent Jim several invitations to join their compact disk issuing clubs. One in the early nineties offered him eight free c.d.s if he promised to buy two more at club prices over the next year. And then he got an offer for ten free if he bought four over two years and so on. The last offer gave him fourteen free c.d.s if he agreed to buy two more over two years.

He accepts the best of these offers, usually ordering mid-1960s country re-issues and anthologies. Consequently, he has quite a stack of c.d.s of forty-year-old music gathering dust in one corner of his living-room—a stack over four feet high. You see, during all the time he was aquiring the recordings, Jim didn't own a c.d. player.

I went with him when he went to shop for one. Apparently he really wanted to hear some George Jones and some Johnny Cash he'd recently acquired, so off we went to find an inexpensive c.d. player.

He told me from the beginning of our shopping trip, "I don't expect to be able to afford a machine with a lot of features, just something that will play one c.d."

"No changer? No programming of individual tracks?" I asked.

"Are you kidding? Let's keep this as simple as we can."

But the least sophisticated c.d. player we could find held five c.d.s at a time and was programed via remote control (included).

A few days later a woman I know told me she'd been over to Jim's for dinner.

"Deer sausage?" I asked.

"Omlets," she replied. "But the reason I brought this up was to tellyou what I saw when I came out of the bathroom after dinner. Jim was sitting in a director's chair across the living room from his stereo. He was leaning forward, listening to the guitar introduction to 'Folsom Prison Blues.' And when those two or three bars were over, he hit a button and the song started again.

"As I stood in the hallway watching, he played that introduction four or five times. I saw he was biting his lower lip as Carl Perkins played, but each time Jim punched the key for a repeat and the music stopped momentarily, he smiled a little and scooted forward in his seat as if to hear the guitar line better still.

"He didn't stop repeating the passage until the guy downstairs began to pound on the ceiling. Then Jim walked across the room to set the remote control down before returning to his chair and obviously enjoying the music."

I visited Jim a few days later and noticed only three c.d.s from the tall stack had so far been opened. And when I left I saw Jim's tenant, a fellow I've known for several years. I said, 'That intro keeps a-playin',/And that's what tortures me.' to him and he grimaced. But then he caught himself and smiled.

Jim used to occasionally host a party on a weekend night close to the summer solstice. That sort of reference to nature appealed to the outdoorsman and to the unreconstructed hippie in him. Certainly "Mr. Natural" was very much at home during these events, usually taking a seat on the front porch rail at the side of his development-enveloped farm house up on Jarvis.

In the dim light coming through the screens from the distant kitchen, his friends would join him in perching on the railing, crinkly plastic cups in their hands, to enjoy the conversation and the smell of the neighborhood's mown grass and banked grill charcoal.

Dozens of the strangest and kindest people would come by these evening at-homes. Sports reporter Steve Brisendine. Poet Ann Carrel. Musician and satirist Brother Jeb. Academics and lawyers, nurserymen and warehousemen, goofs and kinks and raconteurs would wander up and take a seat to talk and drink whatever beer Jim had on offer.

Inside there were joke hors d'oeurves—vienna sausages, synthetically softened "cheese" filled crackers, circus peanuts, and who knows what all else. Usually the cats would get to the snacks long before any of the guests would become so hungry they were willing to ingest the crud.

There would be a little music going in the background (I once made a tape of hits recorded by British rock bands during the years 1964 and 1965, and that played all one party). But most of the sound of one of those wonderful, breezy June gatherings came from the talk and laughter.

I remember one of these occasions when I spent most of the party out in the backyard (still uneven under foot after the official excavation of two years before) talking with a man from Switzerland and a former student of mine about Zoroastrian rituals, a subject I knew little about and about which I retained little I learned during the conversation. Late in the evening, a young woman arrived wearing a short white dress that the Swiss described as a "toga."

As I left the party, perhaps an hour later, the porch was empty and I walked around the side of the house, looking in to see Jim and the toga wearing girl dancing energetically in the empty front room to whatever was playing on the stereo, too low for me to hear. Smiling broadly, Jim had his open hands up, his thumbs to his temples, antler dancing, shifting his head to the right and then to the left.

And that's the way I like to think of him.